Now You See It...

VIVIAN VANDE VELDE

Now You See It...

HARCOURT, INC.

Orlando   Austin   New York   San Diego   Toronto   London

www.HarcourtBooks.com

Library of Congress Cataloging-in-Publication Data
Vande Velde, Vivian.
Now you see it.../by Vivian Vande Velde.
p.   cm.
Summary: With Wendy's new glasses, she begins to see cheerful corpses,
old crones disguised as teenyboppers, and portals to another world—
a place where everyone knows of the glasses' powers and will do anything
they can to get them.
[1. Fantasy.]   I. Title.
PZ7.V2627No   2005
[Fic]—dc22   2004006681
ISBN 0-15-205311-5

Text set in Bembo
Designed by Cathy Riggs

First edition
A C E G H F D B

Printed in the United States of America

For everyone who has ever
resented wearing glasses

CONTENTS

Now You See It...

PROLOGUE

HOW CAN parents who've named their daughter
Wendy ever expect her to be taken seriously?

1

Glasses

One way to look at what happened is that everything is the fault of my optometrist and his enthusiasm for those miserable eye-drops that make your eyes supersensitive to light. But if I've learned one thing from all this, it's that there's generally more than one way to look at anything.

So, from the beginning, a few points to remember:

(1) Without glasses, I can't see farther away than about a foot and a half beyond the tip of my nose.

(2) Glasses may improve someone's *seeing,* but they've never improved anyone's *looks.*

Sure, parents, grandparents, and eyeglass salesmen will assure you that you're cute as a button with your glasses on—*if* what you want to look like is a cute button, though that's not my idea of a big selling point. But in any case, what's the first thing a movie director does to a gorgeous actress when he needs her to look plain for a role?

I've been bugging my mom for contact lenses since about when I was in kindergarten and realized exactly how stupid glasses made me look. That was when I got my first hint that boys don't go for girls who wear glasses—when Nicholas Bonafini, the most popular boy in kindergarten, ran into the LEGO tower I'd spent the last fifteen minutes building, turned around, looked at me, and said, "You're dumb."

It was the glasses, I'm convinced.

Mom is sure I wouldn't take proper care of contact lenses and is worried my eyeballs would rot and fall out as a result. She says I can get contact lenses when I'm eighteen, which is another three years. Eighteen. Big deal. At eighteen, people are considered old enough to vote, move away from home, get a credit card, join the army, and/or get married. Not that anybody wants to marry someone who wears stupid glasses.

(3) I hate those eye doctor eyedrops.

They sting. They make my eyes water, which makes my mascara run, which makes the doctor lecture against the evils of eye makeup (a lecture I've already gotten from Mom). And they make me look stupider than even glasses make me look.

Eye doctors like eyedrops either because you have to be a certifiable sadist to go into the business (I'm convinced that's what half those certificates on their office walls say), or because the drops make your pupils big enough the doctor gets a chance to see to the back of your brain.

While slightly big pupils give girls a kind of doe-eyed innocence, which—while not my first choice—isn't the worst of all possible looks, huge pupils that only leave a tiny rim of iris showing give girls a what-the-heck's-wrong-with-*her*? look that's only appealing to drug pushers and eye doctors.

So the eyedrops sting going in, then they make you look and feel like you're auditioning for a role in *Return of the Mole People,* and—isn't *this* a nice touch?—the effects last a good ten or twelve hours. Even *indoors* in Rochester, New York—where, by the way, gray days were invented—the afternoon light is too bright for someone who's had eyedrops.

Plus, as a bonus side effect, with your pupils that big, your close-up vision evaporates. In fact, you can no longer focus on anything that's closer to you than about a foot and a half away.

Refer back to points one and two.

Sigh.

So, my mother was driving me home from my eye doctor appointment, and I was not pleased. My prescription had not changed, meaning I was stuck with the same ugly glasses I had picked last year. (Yes, I picked them, but how can you tell how bad glasses look when—without the lenses in—you can't see as far away as the mirror? Besides, my mother refuses to buy designer frames, claiming it's against her principles to pay as much for glasses as it would cost to fly the designer to our house to see me in them. My mother is prone to exaggeration.)

I didn't own sunglasses because, in Rochester, there's only about five days in the whole year that you need sunglasses—and the majority of those days are for snow glare rather than actual sunlight. The eye doctor had offered me a pair of construction-paper-and-plastic-film sunglasses about as classy as the ones you get at the 3-D attractions at Disney World, except without the Disney characters. You'd think for what an eye doctor charges, he could give you glasses that don't look as though they cost about fourteen cents a gross.

I'd declined the sunglasses and instead kept my eyes closed as Mom led me out of the doctor's office and to the car. But by the time we pulled into the driveway at home, her patience was wearing thin. She gets that way sometimes. When, as she stopped the car, I told her she might want to seriously consider buying a Seeing Eye dog for me for these annual checkups, she told me to stop sulking.

"No, no, that's all right," I said, flinging my arms up to protect my abused eyeballs from the piercing rays of the sun. "If Helen Keller could manage, I suppose I can, too."

"Oh, Wendy," Mom sighed in a tone like it was my fault I couldn't see. She headed for the house, abandoning me in the front yard.

I staggered across the lawn, alternating between having my eyes tightly closed for maximum protection against the light, and peeking through my fingers for maximum protection against walking into a tree.

The glint of something in the grass caught my attention, which was a wonder no matter how you look at it: I'd given Mom my glasses to carry in her purse, and without them and with my eyes watering I was lucky I could make out my feet.

I leaned over and saw a pair of mirrored sunglasses.

Normally, I would have kept on walking. About 10 percent of the people who wear mirrored sunglasses look really cool. The other 90 percent look like jerks *trying* to look cool.

But I figured that squinting and staggering around the front yard was doing nothing for me in the cool-looks department, anyway, so I picked them up. I knew they didn't belong to anybody in our household. Our household used to consist of me and my mother. Now you have to add my mother's current husband, Bill, and—on a part-time basis—my wicked stepsister, Bill's daughter, Gia. She lives with us during the week and with her mother on weekends. The nicest thing I have to say about her is that I get along best with her on weekends. Our friends— Gia's and my separate friends—all know, as our parents can't quite seem to grasp, that our being the same age is not a *fortunate* coincidence.

We live right across the street from Highland Park, and even though the Lilac Festival wasn't until the following week, a lot of people who are more interested in the lilacs than in the bands and the craft booths and the fried dough come early to beat the crowds. I figured one of these lilac enthusiasts had dropped the sunglasses, and I squinted up and down the sidewalk to see if any likely looking person might have just lost them. Nobody. At least not within my admittedly limited range of sight. So I put them on, figuring that would make finding our front door easier.

My eyeballs were instantly happier. The sunglasses cut out all the glare. And the lenses gave everything a nice pinkish glow, even the statue our next-door neighbor Mrs. Freelander put up by her front stoop in memory of her beloved, dearly departed Pekingese dog of twenty-five years ago, Mr. Tassels. The glasses made the lilacs across the street look stunning. The park has hundreds of varieties of lilacs in shades of dark purple, light purple, bluish purple, pink, and—if I hadn't been wearing those rosy glasses—white. The lenses made them all look gorgeous. I could see an archway among the lilac bushes, which was probably something the festival committee had just put up because I'd never seen it before. It looked like stone though it was more likely granite-colored Styrofoam. Pretty. Everything looked pretty.

"Wendy!" my mother called from inside the house. "Dinner's almost ready!"

I ran up to our front door and was greeted by Bill, who apparently has stronger parental instincts than my own mother, for he seemed to be there specifically to find out what had happened to me.

"Nice shades," he commented, opening the screen door for me.

"Somebody lost them in our front yard," I said.

Mom, heading for the kitchen, detoured to pluck the glasses off my face, saying, "*Eww.* Germs, Wendy." She held them away from her with an expression like she was holding a pooper-scooper bag.

I squinted against the bright light in the front hall and realized, now that the glasses were off my face, that they must have been prescription lenses, and that they must have been pretty close to my own prescription—or I'd never have been able to see Bill, much less the archway across the street.

"Set the table, dear," Mom said, which I guess just went to prove dinner wasn't nearly as almost ready as she'd led me to believe.

"My eyes, my eyes," I groaned, and Bill was the one who took pity on me.

"Gia," he called, "set the table."

"Not my turn," the wicked stepsister yelled back from the living room, where she was getting life tips from the afternoon talk shows.

"Do it anyway," her father said.

Gia came, curling her lip at me when our parents weren't looking. Even without my glasses, I could see *that.*

"Your glasses are in my purse," Mom told me.

But I didn't need them indoors. I was used to getting around the house without the benefit of being able to see much.

I went up to my room and reapplied the mascara the eyedrops had washed away and didn't think again about the sunglasses until the next day.

2

Do You See What I See?

At breakfast the next morning, I poured skim milk into my bowl of cereal—the kind of cereal that's so healthy, all you can taste is the vitamins. The wicked stepsister was eating a warmed cinnamon bun with half a stick of butter melted over the icing: one of the many reasons I hate her. Besides the sexy name, she has a figure like a fashion model; I, on the other hand, have a figure like a duffel bag.

"I'm ready whenever you are," Bill announced to Mom with a meaningful glance at the wall clock. Her car was behind his in the driveway, so she had to leave first, or he had to play musical cars. I'd once pointed out to Mom that life had gotten more com-

plicated when she remarried, but she didn't appreciate my insight.

"Ready," Mom said, though it was obvious she
wasn't. While Bill headed for the garage, she went to
rinse out her coffee cup in the sink. She told me, "I
put your glasses in your backpack."

I knew she was talking to me because, of course,
the wicked stepsister has perfect eyesight.

On the other hand, I was currently wearing my
glasses.

I said, "Was this before or after I put them on this
morning?"

My mother gave me The Look.

Anyone with a mother knows The Look.

She sighed. "Your sunglasses."

For a second I was lost, then I remembered. I'd
had no inclination to keep the mirrored sunglasses I'd
found, or ever to wear them again—they'd been
strictly to get me indoors. Though my pupils were
still slightly dilated this morning, my eyeballs no
longer looked deformed and I figured that, despite
still being a little sensitive to light, I could survive.

"Thanks," I said, anyway.

My mother added, "I disinfected them." Of
course she had. I was lucky she hadn't disinfected me.

"Thanks," I repeated.

She seemed abnormally reluctant to leave.

"Anything wrong?" the wicked stepsister asked.

"No." Finally Mom said what was on her mind: "I'm planning on visiting my mother after work today. Anybody want to meet me there?"

"There" was the nursing home, which we could get to if we took a different bus home, which the school allowed because they knew the situation.

"Sure," the stepsister said. Fine for her: She's planning on going into geriatric nursing—not a career any normal fifteen-year-old aspires to. Besides, she's not related. For her, Nana is a test subject, the same as any other Alzheimer's patient. Gia is a suck-up, trying to impress my mother, because she knows how I hate to go to the nursing home.

"I need to catch up after missing yesterday afternoon's classes," I explained.

"Some other time then," Mom told me mildly. "See you there," she said to Gia. To both of us she added, "Don't be late for your bus," even though she was the one who had struck up the conversation.

Of course the wicked stepsister is beautiful enough she can pull herself together at a moment's notice. I ended up running to the stop after the bus beeped its horn, which was no surprise to me or the bus driver.

I sat in the seat my best friend, Shelley, had saved for me, while the wicked stepsister took the first empty seat because half the kids on the bus are her best friends.

I took my glasses off since Parker Henks gets on the stop after I do. Even though we've been in a lot of the same classes since middle school so he's probably noticed by now that I wear glasses, I always like to look my best for him, whether he glances my way or not.

My backpack was on my lap, my glasses on top of my backpack, and I was talking to Shelley, because I didn't want Parker thinking I was sitting around waiting for him to notice me. Parker didn't even glance in my direction, which might have meant that he really, truly hadn't noticed me or it might have meant that he hadn't noticed me in the same way I hadn't noticed him. But because I wasn't noticing him, it was hard to work out. In any case, he was headed for the back of the bus, followed by three ninth-grade boys who were laughing and poking and shoving one another as they walked down the aisle, and the next thing I knew one of them jostled me, knocking my backpack to the floor.

I looked down just in time to see a size twelve Adidas come down on my glasses.

"Stop!" I yelled, but the guys were still goofing around and I nearly lost my fingers when I reached down.

"See what you've done!" Shelley told them.

I held up my maimed glasses. The lenses were all right, but the arms of the frame were both broken—one cracked but still dangling, the other snapped entirely off—and one of those little whatever-they're-called things that hold the glasses off your nose was smushed flat against the lens.

"Wasn't me," all three of the boys said simultaneously. Each accused another of being the one with big feet and no inkling where he was stepping. Each accused another of starting the shoving. "Duct tape'll fix that," one of them suggested.

The bus driver yelled, "Find a seat!" and the boys moved toward the back of the bus, still spreading the blame around, saying things like, "Wouldn't've happened if she'd been wearing 'em," which was something my parents, too, were sure to point out.

As the bus began moving once again, Shelley asked, "What are you going to do? Will you be able to see if you ask the teachers to let you sit in the front row?"

Like anybody would *ask* to sit in the front row.

"Shelley," I said, "without my glasses, I won't be

able to *find* the front row." Never mind finding the right classrooms. I sighed. "I'm going to have to call my mom and tell her what happened and get her to take me to one of those one-hour eyeglass places." Where the frames cost twice as much. I told Shelley, "My mom's going to kill me."

"No, she won't," Shelley argued. "Statistics show that homicides related to eyewear breakage are actually down this year."

Cute. I gave her the benefit of the doubt and guessed she was trying to make me feel better. I said, "My mother is excitable."

Shelley looked skeptical. "Your dad seems calm and reasonable—he won't let her actually kill you."

"You mean my mother's current husband," I said. I reminded her, "At the moment my dad is living in Hong Kong with the woman formerly known as his secretary."

Shelley rolled her eyes. I think. I was sitting close enough that I'm fairly sure I saw correctly. She said, "Whatever."

Before I could complain that a best friend should be more sympathetic, we were all suddenly thrown forward, with a terrible screech of brakes, and the bus swerved, and we were flung left, then right.

I braced myself for a collision.

Nothing—beyond startled gasps, squeals, and yells, then thuds as assorted kids, backpacks, books, and portable CD players hit the floor.

I bounced between the back of the seat in front of me and my own seat as the bus came to a stop.

"Everybody all right?" the driver shouted.

People were picking themselves up off one another and off the floor.

Those in front were standing to see over the heads of those with seats near the front right-hand windows.

The bus driver didn't wait to see if we all answered that we were okay. "Pedestrian accident near the corner of East and Elmwood," he announced into his two-way radio. He didn't wait for the dispatcher, either, but flung the door open, yelled, "Nobody leave the bus!" then ran outside.

Shelley pushed me out of the seat, and we joined the press of kids at the front.

"What happened?" I asked. By squinting I could make out a crowd of people on the street corner, all looking in the direction of the intersection, where there was a smaller cluster of people crouched or kneeling on the asphalt. The bus had stopped in the middle of the street, at a diagonal. "Did we hit someone?"

Somehow I'd ended up near Gia, the wicked stepsister, and she answered, "No, somebody else did."

I squinted harder but really couldn't make anything out, which was probably all for the best.

Those at the windows leaned out and shouted to the people on the sidewalk. The story, as near as I could make out from too many people talking at once, was that a car coming from the opposite direction had tried to beat the bus through the intersection to make a left-hand turn—apparently not seeing the lady crossing the side street.

Our bus driver shoved his way back onto the bus, past the kids who were crowding the doorwell. He ignored all the questions, grabbed the first-aid kit, then warned again, "Nobody leave the bus."

After five minutes that seemed like forever, sirens approached, first a couple of police cars, then an ambulance.

"Is she going to be all right?" Gia called out to our bus driver as he came to stand by the bus now that the ambulance guys had arrived.

"I'm sure she'll be fine," our driver said. "But the police want to talk to me as a witness, so I need to get you another bus."

We pointed out that we were two short blocks

from school, but he ignored us and got on the radio to speak with the dispatcher. We were all crowding the front of the bus, so we all heard the dispatcher say that another bus could pick us up, and we all heard him say it would be in about twenty minutes, depending on traffic. Judging from how the traffic around us wasn't moving, we all knew we could add at least another ten minutes to that estimate. Even with the windows open, we were beginning to get sweaty and cranky in the May heat. We complained, loudly, that we were within two minutes' walk of school, with only one side street to cross, and the youngest of us were in ninth grade.

Our logic, or our whining, finally worked, and our driver told us we could go, if we all stuck together and went straight to school. We all vowed on our honor.

"Think you can make it without your glasses?" Shelley asked me as the bus emptied around us, everyone having already forgotten that sticking-together promise.

Walking around without glasses in your own home is totally different from walking around on the street without being able to see, but what choice did I have?

Which was when inspiration struck. "Hold on," I said, suddenly remembering my mother saying she'd put yesterday's sunglasses in my backpack. "Wait till you see these."

I found them in the little front zippered section, tracking them down by sniffing for the scent of Lysol.

"Whoa!" Shelley said, knowing that mirrored sunglasses—with or without the smell—weren't my usual style.

"But they're prescription lenses," I told her. I put them on, and once again everything took on a pink glow. Still, everything came into focus, too. "Shelley!" I exclaimed, feigning sudden recognition. "It's you!" Then I asked, "Do they look too awful?"

Shelley shrugged.

Okay, well then, I'd take them off as soon as I got to school and wasn't in danger from traffic.

The bus was empty now, except for the two of us, and I glanced out the window to assure myself that Parker Henks wasn't in the vicinity. He was halfway down the block already, with a group that included my wicked stepsister. The closest kid was Julian York, who'd paused just beyond the crowd of accident onlookers to readjust his backpack. Nobody had stopped to wait for him, either. Julian was new this year, and I'd never really talked to him beyond "Hi" and "Mind if I move this chair to that table?" and "What page did Mrs. McDermott say to turn to?" He'd struck me, back in September, as too tall and too skinny, but now after eight months of not really looking at him, I said to Shelley, "Hmm, Julian's not half bad looking," trying to sound Shelley out to see what she thought.

Shelley raised her eyebrows at me. "Maybe you better not depend on those glasses too much," she suggested.

In any case, he had moved on by the time we stepped off the bus. Shelley asked, "Do you really think that lady will be all right, or was our driver just telling us that because we're kids?"

Over the heads of the crouching ambulance attendants, I saw the accident victim sit up. "Well, I guess that answers that," I said.

"What?" Shelley asked.

"She's sitting up."

Shelley stood on tiptoe but must have been at a bad angle, because apparently she still couldn't see. She asked, "Really?"

The woman got up.

"Geez," I said. "You'd think they wouldn't let her do that."

"What?" Shelley asked.

Though the woman looked about sixty or so and was wearing a flowered dress, maybe Shelley mistook her for one of the ambulance attendants, because

Shelley was still craning her neck, trying to get a better look at the stretcher the ambulance guys had set down, while the woman was walking away.

I was amazed that no one tried to stop her, to tell her, "Let us check you out, just in case you're lightheaded or something." But they weren't even looking at her. Everyone ignored her totally. She walked through the crowd, right up to me.

"Are you an angel?" she asked, which seemed proof to me that she was confused enough to need medical attention.

"No." I was too surprised to ask her if she was sure she should be walking. Her dress was smudged from lying in the street, and her knees and one elbow were scraped, but that was the only blood on her.

Except, I suddenly noticed, for a slight red dribble from her right ear that stuck a wisp of her gray hair to her cheek.

"What?" Shelley asked, distracted, still facing the intersection, as though she had not heard the woman's question but only my answer.

The woman looked around. "Oh," she said. "Sorry. My mistake." She started walking toward a patch of light on the sidewalk so bright that even with my sunglasses I couldn't look straight at it. The woman walked into the light, then turned to wave good-bye to me, smiled the most beautiful smile I've ever seen, and dissolved. A moment later the light also dissolved.

I grabbed Shelley's arm. "Shelley"—my voice, once I got it to work, was quavering—"did you see that?"

"I'm afraid so," she answered. But she didn't seem nearly as freaked out as she should have been. In fact, she *still* wasn't even looking in the right direction.

I looked back at where the ambulance attendants were lifting the stretcher to put it back into the ambulance—the stretcher, with a blanket covering a still form beneath it.

"Wow," Shelley said in a shaky whisper, "she must have died while we were standing here watching."

3

Vroom, Vroom

I whipped those glasses off my face faster than if there had been a cute boy in the vicinity.

"What?" Shelley asked me, but she was still mostly watching the ambulance guys. She probably thought I was trying to avoid seeing any details, not realizing I'd already seen way too many.

The thing was, I knew what I'd seen. There was no use in trying to convince myself that I was dreaming or that the glasses had caused some sort of distortion. I had seen a ghost, a spirit, whatever you want to call a dead person who's up and walking. Talking, too, though apparently Shelley hadn't heard. Whoever heard of glasses improving your hearing?

But seeing the dead lady wasn't the worst of it.

When I took the glasses off, the person standing next to Shelley disappeared. I don't mean, *disappeared* as in "became too fuzzy to make out." *Shelley* had become fuzzy, but I could still see her well enough to be able to know it was her. I could even make out the movement of the paramedics putting the stretcher that held the body of the dead woman into the ambulance. But there was no trace of the person who'd been standing right next to Shelley.

I couldn't help myself. Scared as I was, I put the glasses back on. Looking, when my better sense warned me not to. Like poking at a zit that you just know is only going to get worse for the poking, but you stupidly can't resist.

Yep, someone was definitely there who wasn't there when I wasn't wearing the glasses.

He was dressed in a suit and carried a briefcase— a youngish business executive or lawyer is what he looked like. While I had the glasses on, he was just one of the many walking to work who had paused to rubberneck an accident.

He turned, slowly, as though he'd become aware that I was staring at him. He kind of leaned in and gave a little wave at me, the way you do when you're trying to get the attention of someone you suspect is too distracted to notice you.

I backed away.

"You can see me!" he said, sounding delighted.

I must have looked scared because he asked, "What, am I beginning to leak or something?"

He'd been fine a moment before, but as soon as he asked, the left side of his head caved in, and the front of his shirt grew bloody.

My breath escaped in an involuntary hiss.

He set the briefcase down and readjusted his head. The blood faded and disappeared. "Sometimes," he explained, "when I forget to concentrate—"

I took the glasses off again, and he disappeared and I could no longer hear his voice.

Which was no good, because I knew he was there, whether or not I could see him. You can't undo knowledge.

I put the glasses back on.

"...fast cars," the man was saying to me, "*vroom, vroom*. Everybody in a hurry. That's what happened to me. Except, of course, in my case I was the one doing the hurrying. A bit of advice for you: Never get into an argument with an SUV. Just the same," he went on, "it's fascinating. As they say: Like not being able to take your eyes off a car wreck." Then, sounding just like Shelley, he asked, "What?" and patted himself on the chest area. "Is the steering wheel column sticking out again?"

I was having trouble breathing. If it hadn't been for all the now-you-see-it/now-you-don't nonsense with the glasses, I would have assumed that the reason I was able to see dead people was because I, myself, was currently on the boundary of life and death, dying of a heart attack. Not, of course, that I would be having a heart attack except for what I was seeing. I managed to squeak out, "Why are you still here?" since the lady had walked into the light only moments after dying.

While the dead lawyer or accountant or whatever he was paused to consider, Shelley assumed that I was speaking to her. "You're right," she said with a heavy sigh. "We should be heading off to school. I wish we'd gone without seeing that, so we'd still think that poor lady had survived."

But the dead guy hadn't been considering: He'd been concentrating. "Listen!" he told me. "A siren. I bet there's been another accident. I'm going to go take a look." He picked up his briefcase and took off at a fast pace, not quite running, as though mindful of keeping a dignified appearance despite his excitement.

"Wait!" I said.

The dead guy ignored me, and Shelley said, "What is it, Wendy? You're acting weird, you know that?"

Yet again I took the glasses off. I tried handing them to her. "See that guy?" I asked.

"Which?"

Of course she wouldn't be able to see him until she put the glasses on, and in the time it would take me to explain, he'd be lost in the crowd. Then Shelley would look at me like I was crazy instead of just weird.

Maybe there were more dead people in the crowd, which I could find out by looking around *with,* then *without,* my glasses. That was assuming that dead people as a class were curious about car accidents, and that it wasn't just this one guy because that was how he'd died.

Or maybe there weren't any dead people at all. Maybe my mind had taken a sharp turn into a different time zone, the way my grandmother's had.

There are some things you can't tell, even to a best friend.

I wiped the sunglasses on the hem of my shirt, as though that was why I'd taken them off.

"Never mind," I said.

4

An Even-Worse-than-Usual
Day at School

As I walked along with Shelley, pretending my world hadn't suddenly taken a detour into the bizarre, I tried to look attentive while she chattered about how we'd better hurry up because we were going to be significantly later than the other late kids. I was only half listening, thinking.

What I was thinking was that I had two questions: Who in the world had made these glasses? And why?

They had to be some kind of brand-new high-tech scientific breakthrough, I decided. Probably part of a secret government project, because there certainly hadn't been anything in the news about such a discovery. I knew that for a fact because Bill, my mother's current husband, thought world events made a suitable topic for supper-table conversation. He knew I never watched anything but movies and MTV, and Gia, the wicked stepsister, got her news from afternoon TV. Bill wanted us to be well-informed members of society. And he certainly hadn't mentioned anything about glasses that let you see dead people.

And wherever the glasses were originally from, how had they ended up on my front lawn?

Okay, okay, that's three questions—math isn't my best subject.

Whatever. The more I thought about that last question, the more I doubted my previous conclusion.

Those glasses didn't look like the kind of thing you would expect a bunch of scientists to make in their first attempt to peek into the afterlife. *I* would expect such a device to look like heavy-duty goggles, not like the kind of cheesy fashion attire you could find at the dollar store. Even as I saw Shelley looking in my direction to make sure I was paying attention, even as we passed other people on the street who didn't glance at me, I thought: *These glasses were meant to avoid attracting attention.*

I, of course, did not want to attract attention, either—and I most certainly didn't want to see dead people. I simply wanted to be able to make it through the school day without walking into walls or falling down stairs, neither of which was a sure thing with my own unaided vision. My mother would be mad enough about the broken frames if we had to go get a new pair after dinner; I did *not* want to call her at work and ask her to drop everything to come pick me up now because I couldn't tell which way faced front in my classrooms.

At the office, Mrs. Pincelli, the secretary, gave us late passes—after giving us her fishy eye for straggling in after all the other kids on our bus had managed to come in within a couple minutes of one another. But Mrs. Pincelli isn't happy unless she's able to give the fishy eye to *some*body about *some*thing, so I didn't take it to heart.

"You going to be okay?" Shelley asked as we left our backpacks in our lockers and got out the books we'd need for morning classes. She had English lit first period; I had to go to biology on the second floor.

"I'll be fine," I told her. "Actually, these lenses let me see just as well as my regular glasses." I still didn't mention the bonus special effects.

Shelley asked, "Even indoors?"

That was another question, now that she pointed

it out: Why didn't the sunglasses darken the indoors the way normal sunglasses would have?

"I'll be okay," I assured her.

"Even with Mrs. Robellard?" Shelley pressed, though now she was grinning.

Mrs. Robellard, we had figured out long ago, must have inhaled the fumes of too many embalmed frogs over her thirty or forty years as biology teacher at James Fenimore Cooper High. There was speculation that the jar that sat on the back shelf and was labeled PICKLED PIG'S HEART really contained her own.

"See you at lunch," I said, and started toward the stairs. At least the halls were deserted, just in case I had to take the glasses off. Of course, I wouldn't be inclined to take them off unless I started seeing dead people again; and I assumed there wouldn't be too many of those hanging around the school halls.

Even on the second floor, where—with most of the classroom doors closed—it's creepily dim, I could see perfectly well.

Then I opened the door to room 237.

The windows were open because it was such a warm day, and my late pass fluttered on top of my books like it was seriously toying with the idea of flying away and sending me running off to chase it all across the classroom.

When I looked up after slapping down that skittish late pass so it couldn't get away, I saw the ugliest person in the world straightening up from leaning over the desk at the front of the room. I thought, *Either something truly bizarre has happened to Mrs. Robellard or we have the Wicked Witch of the West as a substitute teacher today.*

This woman had gray and stringy hair that hung down to her shoulders. Her nose was crooked. And could it possibly be? Yes, definitely: a wart at the tip. The eyes were red rimmed, with the whites more yellow than white. And malevolent as she glared at me.

There's old. There's ugly. There's mean. But this went beyond that. The woman standing by the desk gave new meaning to the expression "made my skin crawl."

"Well, Wendy. How nice of you to grace us with your presence."

There was the scrape of a chair, and I saw Mrs. Robellard get up from behind the desk and step around the witchy-looking person to confront me.

Well, for good or ill, at least the newcomer hadn't shoved her into an oven and eaten her.

"I, I, I..." I couldn't get any further than that, so I just handed her the note.

While the hideous stranger glowered at the interruption, Mrs. Robellard gave a suspicious "Hmph!" then said, "Do you have a late pass for your homework, too?"

"No," I managed to mumble, and I got my homework out from between the pages of the biology book. Because the book is a bit shorter than a sheet of paper, the bottom edge was crumpled.

Mrs. Robellard eyed the page dubiously. "You may take your seat," she told me because I was just standing there, gawking at the other woman, at the way her dry, wrinkled skin, dotted with nasty age spots, hung loose from her arms. I thought, *If I was that old, I'd wear long sleeves, regardless of the weather.* But this woman had on a little spaghetti-strap top as though she was the age of the students and not about a hundred years old. Beneath the top, her boobs— *She isn't wearing a bra!* I realized in horror—drooped nearly to her waist.

"Wendy." Mrs. Robellard's voice was sharp. "Sit down. Read chapter twelve. Quiz starts at a quarter after. And take off those sunglasses. We are not in Hollywood."

"Ahm," I said, "I broke my other pair. These are prescription lenses."

"If you say so." She'd seen me wearing glasses from September to May, but she curled her lip suspiciously. Then she waved me to my seat, and sat back down at her desk to resume her conversation with the old witch woman.

I took my seat, but I couldn't stop staring at the class visitor. I leaned to my right, to Franklin Yeager, since Tiffanie Mills, who normally sits in front of me, apparently wasn't in today.

"Who's that?" I hissed to Franklin.

"Who?" Franklin whispered back as though there was more than one new person in the class.

"With Mrs. Robellard."

Franklin gave me his version of Mrs. Pincelli's fishy look. "You mean Tiffanie?" he asked.

"No," I said in disgust and inclined my head toward the front of the room, toward the desk. I know Mrs. Robellard is old herself and not exactly on the attractive side, but how could she stand to have her face so close to that other woman's?

Franklin just shrugged and shook his head and went back to the reading.

Tiffanie? What in the world was he talking about, Tiffanie? Tiffanie wasn't even in today. He must have misunderstood my question. I wondered what he thought I'd asked: *Who's the best-looking person in the school? Who's the most popular? Who do all the girls wish they were, and all the boys wish they could date?*

Something, however, made me push my glasses down my nose a bit, to squint over the top.

Sure enough, heading back to the desk in front of mine after finishing her talk with Mrs. Robellard, wearing that same spaghetti-strapped little red top, was Tiffanie Mills.

5

A Bad Day Gets Worse

Tiffanie Mills is the most popular girl at James Fenimore Cooper High, so she isn't what I'd call a personal friend. That was probably the only thing that saved me from screaming "Tiffanie! What happened to you?" and making a total moron of myself. Which is good, because my status at school is already semimoron, and I wouldn't have liked to have committed myself completely to the camp that includes those kids who are most likely to end up working at fast-food franchises or being featured on *America's Most Wanted*.

I checked out the other kids. Nobody else seemed affected by my glasses, just Tiffanie.

I only dropped my biology book once before I got it opened in front of me on the desk. I had no idea which chapter Mrs. Robellard had said to read, and probably was incapable of finding it, anyway, so I just flipped the pages till I was about halfway into the book, and then pretended to read.

What in the world was going on with Tiffanie?

I glanced up once more, first over the tops of my glasses, then through the lenses. Tiffanie was just flouncing into her seat in front of me.

Believe me, flouncing takes on a whole new meaning when it's done by someone who looks like your great-grandmother wearing strappy sandals, a skimpy skirt, and no bra.

The back of Tiffanie's chair jostled solidly against my desk.

Tiffanie was not a ghost. The other dead people I'd seen—amazing how quickly that begins to roll off the tongue— The other dead people I'd seen were different. Without the glasses, there had been no sign of the businessman. Without the glasses, the woman who'd been run over just lay on the street until she was carried away by the ambulance crew. If Tiffanie was dead, other people shouldn't be seeing her. And in any case, she shouldn't look like a hundred-year-old crone. What kind of death could have caused her to look like that? Severe inhalation of toxic hair spray? Allergic reaction to lip liner?

"Wendy," Tiffanie whispered.

Through the lenses, I could see her drumming her fingertips on my desk: perfectly sculpted passionberry red nails at the ends of pale, arthritis-gnarled fingers.

I didn't raise my head but looked at her beautiful self up over the rims of my glasses. She'd twisted in her seat just enough that she could recover herself quickly if Mrs. Robellard glanced this way. In a hushed voice, Tiffanie asked, "Got a nail file?" She extended her index finger, which might or might not have had some tiny imperfection.

Just look at her OVER the glasses, I told myself. Still, I had to swallow before I could manage an "Um, sorry."

"Okay," Tiffanie said in a tone that indicated she wouldn't hold this against me. She started to face forward, then turned back again. "Wendy," she whispered.

"What?"

"You're reading your book upside down." She gave her patented crinkled-nose smile at me. I was just grateful I didn't see *that* through the lenses.

"Thanks," I whispered to get her to turn back in her seat.

Mrs. Robellard stood and announced, "All right, books away. Get out a clean sheet of paper and pen."

People groaned because she had said the quiz would be at a quarter after and it was only twelve after. Of course, everyone would have groaned in any case: There's never enough time to cram for a quiz when you haven't been paying attention in class. What was this unit about again? Oh yeah, dinosaurs. They couldn't have given this to us when we were eight and interested?

Next to me, Faith Wickstrum was rummaging around in her purse. I knew she was looking for her MarineLand pen, the one with the dolphins on it. Earlier in the year, she had been using it when she aced a geometry test she hadn't studied for, so she figured the pen was lucky, and now she always used it for tests and quizzes.

All of a sudden, two tiny little creatures appeared. They looked like little men, except for the fact that they were about three inches tall, and they were that shade of eye-bedazzling blue that the manufacturers of Popsicles and Kool-Aid call blue raspberry. I don't know if they just materialized out of thin air or if they crawled out of, or up from, or down from somewhere—but suddenly they were on Faith's desk.

"Get it, get it, get it!" one shouted in a shrill little voice as the other dived headfirst into Faith's purse.

My biology book must have fallen from my numb fingers, because I heard the thud as it hit the floor. Mrs. Robellard probably gave me a dirty look, but all my attention was on the two little guys.

"Got it!" I heard a muffled little voice proclaim. I saw the top of his tiny head poking out from the front pocket of Faith's purse. His hair looked like purple faux fur, and he was wearing clothes that seemed to have been manufactured from leaves and birds' nests. "Here you go." He handed Faith's lucky dolphin pen off to the other guy. I would have thought that they'd have trouble managing, since the pen was so much longer than they were tall, but they must have been stronger than they looked.

"Look out!" the first guy warned as Faith, who apparently couldn't see these guys—or her pen— moved her hand to search another compartment of her purse. She appeared totally oblivious to them, even as she knocked one back into her purse, and the other teetered on the edge of her desk, holding the pen like a high-wire artist trying to get his balance.

From inside the purse came muffled squeaks, squawks, and cries of "Hey!" "Watch it!" "Don't get so personal!" as Faith felt around for her pen.

Suspicious, I lowered my sunglasses down my nose. Sure enough, the little blue whatever-he-was disappeared. I couldn't see the pen, either.

"Miss Wickstrum!" Mrs. Robellard asked impatiently. "Are you ready to begin the quiz?"

"I'm looking for my pen," Faith explained, resuming her search where she had already checked. "I know it's got to be here someplace."

"Hey, Guido!" the little blue guy on the desk called out to his companion. "You okay?" His voice was thin and high, like when you fast-forward a tape.

"Sure, I'm okay," the second little guy said, climbing out of the purse, though his purple hair was all pointing backward as though he'd been caught in a mighty wind. Seeing the other guy still doing his balancing act with the pen, he warned, "Hey, don't drop that thing, or she'll be able to see it."

"I won't drop it," the first guy complained. "Whadyathink I am? Clumsy, like you?"

"Who you calling 'clumsy,' butterfingers?" The second guy launched himself at the first and they began rolling around on the desk.

And all the while, Faith kept searching, searching.

I finally remembered to close my mouth.

Mrs. Robellard sighed. "Does anyone have an

extra pen so Miss Wickstrum can take the chapter twelve quiz along with the rest of us?"

"But...," Faith protested feebly. In a last-ditch effort, she dumped the contents of her purse out on her desk, scattering lip gloss, hairpins, sticks of gum, small change, and scraps of paper which may or may not have been fortune-cookie fortunes.

The two bickering blue guys screamed as the deluge of stuff buried them, but it was the kind of scream you give on a roller coaster, so I doubted they were seriously injured.

Mrs. Robellard said icily, "Miss Wickstrum," and Faith sighed and accepted the pen Franklin Yeager was offering her: an olive green one whose top bore Franklin's teeth prints, and on which was inscribed MONDO TRUCK RALLY/SEPTEMBER 21–28.

Faith held her purse open and swept the pile of stuff off her desk back in, little blue men and all.

"Question number one," Mrs. Robellard announced, and so the quiz began.

Well, one thing the glasses didn't have any effect on was whether I could keep straight what had happened in the Cretaceous versus Jurassic eras.

While I was glancing around the room hoping for help from some of the posters on the walls, I saw the two little men crawling out of Faith's purse, which she had hung off the back of her seat. They seemed to have resolved their differences, for one reached down to give the other a hand up.

"Did you lick it good, Guido?" the first guy asked in his high helium voice.

"Licked it real good," the second guy assured him. "When she finds it, it'll be all covered with purse lint."

The two guys jumped off the back of Faith's chair, landing lightly despite the fact that, for their height, that had to be like jumping off a minor mountain. They ran up to the front of the room, climbed Mrs. Robellard's desk, and knocked a couple papers into the nearby trash can, laughing all the while. Except, of course, when one said something the other didn't like, which would get them pinching and poking and throwing punches until they lost track of what it was they'd been arguing about and went off to do more mischief. Even the fact that they were targeting Mrs. Robellard didn't make me like them any better: They were just plain mean.

Sitting in the back row, I had a good view of them as they untied Sean Park's shoelaces, pulled the back off one of Peg Denzler's earrings, and kicked a quarter under the baseboard heater where it would never be found.

Come on. Come close to me, I mentally dared them. I don't know if they could tell I could see them or if they just found too many others to torment before they got to me, but about the time the quiz was ending, they heard the janitor pushing the restroom cleaning cart out in the hallway and took off after her, laying in plans for flushing away all the toilet paper and jamming the Kotex machine.

As we were handing our papers up to the front of the classroom, I raised my hand.

"Miss Selmeyer?" Mrs. Robellard sighed at me.

"I'm feeling kind of funny," I said. *Kind of?* I was seeing dead people and blue guys.

"'Funny,'" she echoed.

I put my hands over my stomach.

"Will the ladies' room suffice, or do you need to see the nurse?"

I didn't want to go to the nurse, but I didn't want to go to the ladies' room if those two blue nasties were tearing the place apart.

"Nurse, I think," I said weakly.

Mrs. Robellard sighed. "It was nice having you while we did." She scrawled a pass for me.

When I went to take it, she held on to it for an extra moment. "Don't think I'll make allowances for this on the quiz," she warned.

I wanted to say, *I'd never expect you to make allowances for anything.* But I didn't have the nerve.

6

Some Guys Need Magic Glasses to Look Cute

The nurse wasn't in her office.

Because of a tight school budget, we'd long shared a nurse with the middle school, so that Mrs. Starr was here Monday, Wednesday, and Friday mornings and Tuesday and Thursday afternoons. But ever since the last round of school budget cuts, when they added visiting one of the elementary schools to her itinerary, her schedule had become too complicated for me to figure out. Or maybe there was no pattern. Maybe she just showed up wherever she wanted, waiting for psychic vibes to drop hints which school's student body was most likely to suffer a medical emergency at any given time.

In any case, the note taped to her door said:

m.s. only this pm, weds. am, thurs. am,
fri. pm til 2.
Longridge except tues.

Mrs.

I had no idea what that meant, but the door was locked, so it probably meant "not here now."

The nurse's office is in a quiet little dead-end hall on the first floor, located beyond the north wing set of stairs. So I just plunked myself down on the floor, leaning my back against the office door as though expecting Mrs. Starr to be back momentarily. I pushed the glasses up into my hair and rested my face against my knees.

Had the world just gotten weird, or had it always been and I was only now seeing it?

Okay, I thought, *the glasses let me see into the after-life—that's why I could see those two ghosts.*

That almost made sense: Scientists might have invented a means to glimpse at someone's postdeath... what? Soul? Psychic energy? Whatever.

But what about Tiffanie?

Well, maybe I was seeing into the future, seeing what she would look like in another eighty-five to ninety years or so. Not anybody else, of course—just Tiffanie Mills. Sure. *That* was a useful tool that science was just waiting for someone to invent.

And what about those two little blue guys with the personality deficiency? Aliens? Perhaps scientists—guessing the world had been invaded by malevolent invisible-to-earthlings beings—had developed a technology to enable us to see them. . . .

But that was hardly reasonable: Aliens traveling from light-years away, taking who-could-guess-how-long to cross countless galaxies, braving unknown dangers . . . all to lick Faith Wickstrum's lucky MarineLand pen and trash James Fenimore Cooper High's second-floor ladies' room?

Maybe I groaned, but—if so—just the tiniest bit. And maybe I was rocking back and forth like one of the special-needs kids coming off her meds, but that was just to keep from groaning. I was feeling so miserable, I didn't even register the sound of footsteps coming down the nearby stairs until they reached the bottom.

I *had* just registered that they'd stopped rather than gone on when someone asked, "You all right?"

By squinting, I was able to make out Julian York. He was carrying a pile of papers, so I gathered he was running some errand for some teacher, and I was just plain lucky that he had chosen this particular staircase to use.

"I'm okay," I told him.

He rocked back and forth a bit himself, maybe inwardly debating whether to accept that answer and continue on his way.

"Really," I assured him.

Obviously I did a superb job of hiding my distress. He came and sat down on the floor next to me. "Did you hit your head?" he asked.

Actually, a head injury would explain a lot.

I touched my face around the hairline, expecting my fingers to come away sticky, thinking, *Shelley, you could have mentioned that I had an open head wound.* "Where?" I asked, remembering the dead businessman asking, *What, am I beginning to leak or something? Is the steering wheel column sticking out again?*

"We all bounced around quite a bit," Julian said. "Backpacks were flying through the air. Things happened too fast to know *what* was happening."

I came to suspect he was asking in a general sort of way if I was hurt because of what we'd been through—*not* because of a blood-gushing wound.

Julian must have caught on that I wasn't touching my scalp because I was checking for lice. He said, "You *look* fine." He gave a slow, warm smile that was sweet enough that even an insecure girl like me could take it as he meant it when he added, "Except, of course, for the fact that you look terrible."

"Oh, well, in that case, thank you very much," I told him.

Sitting this close, I could see that I'd been wrong in thinking, when I'd glimpsed him getting off the bus, that he was better looking than I had originally thought. He was too thin and his hair was thin, too, and a bit scraggly; its lightish brownish blondish color could best be described as *faded*. And his cheekbones were too prominent and his nose skinny and long. And yet I'd been right, too: It wasn't so much that his skin, though pale, was luminous; or that his eyes were a beautiful shade of green; or that his teeth were white and even. It was his expression—he was genuinely concerned—and that's hard to resist.

He said, "I once got smacked in the head, and to this day don't exactly remember it happening. I kept telling people I was fine, but they could tell I was losing track of what I was saying halfway through and was too confused to even know I was confused. It was only when my trainer felt my head—and made me feel it—that we found this big, bloody bump. It only started hurting after that."

Trainer? I wouldn't have picked Julian as the athletic type. He certainly wasn't on any of JFC's sports teams. Maybe at his old school—since he'd only been here since September. Or at his middle school. "Soccer injury?" I guessed. Everyone plays soccer in middle school. Even *I* had played soccer in middle school.

He froze, as though startled, and I thought maybe he *had been* a jock at his old high school—swimming or lacrosse or some sport we didn't have. Maybe he was even insulted that I had fallen back on that old standby, soccer. But then he said, "Um, yeah."

Maybe he'd been considering. Maybe he really couldn't remember *anything* about it.

Because, of course, there wasn't any reason I could think of why he'd want to lie about playing soccer.

"I'm just saying," he told me, "if you're feeling queasy or something, maybe you hit your head." He added, "Though your pupils look fine. You don't feel sleepy, do you?"

"No more than during any other first-period class," I told him.

He grinned, then glanced at the note on Mrs. Starr's door. "She won't be back till this afternoon," he said, and I had no idea if he was able to interpret her code or was just guessing. "Do you mind?"

I didn't know what he was asking until he set down the papers he'd been holding, knelt in front of me, and set his hands on my head. The sunglasses were in the way and our hands collided as he and I both reached for them at the same time. I hung them from the neckline of my shirt, and he felt all over my head.

"This feels stupid," I said.

"No, it doesn't," he countered.

And actually, he was right. It felt kind of sexy. Like having a male hairdresser massage your head. Except with the guy who cuts my hair, I *know* he's not interested. *Could* Julian York be interested in me? And was I interested in having him be interested in me? Maybe. Definitely...maybe. At least *maybe* enough that I was glad I'd washed and conditioned my hair last night so that my hair smelled like apricots instead of—heaven forbid—hair.

He was leaning close, his eyes unfocused as he concentrated, his fingers moving slowly and gently over my scalp. "I don't feel anything," he told me.

"Maybe you should keep looking," I said, shocking myself with how brazen I was.

He sat back on his heels, laughing. "You're definitely looking better," he told me.

"I'm okay," I told him. "I really don't think anything smacked me on the head. It's just..." Hmm, maybe I should just open up and tell this sweet guy that I've been seeing dead people, witchy people, and blue people.

Yeah, right.

I finished, "It's just that lady died."

"Probably," Julian agreed. "It didn't look good."

I realized he'd left—everyone had left, except for me and Shelley—before the ambulance guys had covered her up.

I found myself saying, "No. I saw her."

Hard to tell what to make of Julian's face.

Waiting, I guess, to see what I'd say next.

And there was no way I could tell a virtual stranger what had been going on.

I finished, "They pulled the blanket up over her face, and they put her in the ambulance, and they left without turning their siren on."

"Rough," Julian acknowledged, meaning, I think, *rough* that I had witnessed it, because *rough* is obviously an inadequate word for dying. "Maybe you should ask to see Mr. Harman?"

Mr. Harman is the school psychologist, whose schedule is tougher to figure out than Mrs. Starr's: He doesn't even leave notes on his door; he's just there or, more often, not.

I shook my head.

"Want to come with me to the office?" He picked up his papers. "Talk to Mr. Rajamani?"

Mr. Rajamani, our principal, is actually a pretty good guy. But that didn't mean I wanted to talk to him. "No," I said. "I'd better be heading back to Mrs. Robellard's class."

He gave a pained expression. "Ah," he said as though that explained everything, "you're coming from Mrs. Robellard's class." Then, more seriously, "Are you sure you're okay?"

I nodded, and he stood, which moved him out of the range in which I could see him clearly. But I could see him extend a hand to help me get to my feet.

He hauled me up to a vertical position, then asked, "Still okay?"

"Absolutely."

"Tell someone if you're feeling poorly," he said, sounding like an adult, and an old-fashioned one at that.

I saluted him, trying to be spontaneous and playful, only realizing just as my hand went up what a geeky move that was. But he saluted back, making the gesture cute rather than geeky. Then he picked up his papers and started walking away from me down the hall.

Why didn't I leave well enough alone?

But he'd been so nice, I wanted one more glimpse of him.

So I plucked the sunglasses off my shirt and put them on.

He turned back once more, which was sweet, as though wanting to make sure I was all right, and I waved. He waved back, though hesitantly, probably wondering about the sunglasses, since he wasn't in Mrs. Robellard's first-period class and hadn't heard about my breaking my regular glasses.

Wow, I thought. *What's the matter with me? He really IS good-looking.*

He faced back around and headed for the office, and that was when I noticed: His ears were long and pointed. I would have seen them—I would have *had* to have seen them—if they'd been there before, while he'd been kneeling in front of me feeling for evidence of a cracked skull.

So these glasses let me see dead people still walking and talking, they let me see the gorgeous Tiffanie Mills looking like a century-old crone, they let me see blue guys who delighted in mayhem, and they let me see Julian York looking better then he did when I wasn't wearing the glasses, if you didn't mind ears that made him look like he was a refugee from a *Star Trek* convention.

All in all, I would have felt better if I'd really had a concussion.

7

Conspiracy

I decided I'd been mature about this long enough: It was time to call my mother and ask her to come pick me up right away on account of my blindness. Best not to mention the possible mental aberration. Not wanting to catch sight of any more weirdness, I took off the glasses and felt my way to the pay phone, down by the gym.

When I dialed my mother's work number, her voice mail came on and told me she was in the Syracuse office for the day. Syracuse is slightly over an hour and a half away. She probably hadn't even arrived there yet. I tried to picture myself leaving a message for her to please turn right around and drive another hour and a half back to pick me up from school because I'd broken my glasses.

Hmmm. Naw, that wasn't something I wanted to picture.

The recording went on to tell me that if this was an emergency and I needed to speak to someone in person, I was to dial Paula at extension 335.

Considering I'd never met Paula, I decided she wasn't likely to pick me up, either.

I was desperate enough to call my mother's current husband, Bill. The guy who answered said Bill was away from his desk and asked, "Is this his daughter?"

Geez, a trick question. I said, "Uhh, this is Wendy." Let this guy make up his own mind about the relationship.

He said, "Wendy, he's doing performance appraisals in building fifty-four. Do you need me to get him?"

I remembered Bill obsessing about this at dinner the last couple nights. Performance appraisals are like report cards for the workers at his company, and Bill—being a supervisor—is like the teacher handing the report cards out.

Probably not exactly a good time to interrupt him.

"When will he be through?" I asked.

"One o'clock," the guy told me. "Then he's

meeting our supervisor for lunch and to get *his* p.a. So, probably around two o'clock. Should I have him call you?"

School would be almost over by then.

"No, it's nothing important." Surely the lie came through in my voice.

If so, this guy didn't have kids or wasn't good at picking up nuances—someone should probably mention that in *his* p.a. "Okay," he said, and hung up.

I wouldn't meet up with Shelley till lunch, but I worked out a plan: Without explaining why—just in case I *was* simply losing my mind—I would have her try on the glasses while Julian and Tiffanie were in view. If they looked to Shelley the way they looked to me, that would prove something...though *what,* exactly, I wasn't sure.

Of course, Shelley would need convincing to even try the glasses on. She would point out that she didn't wear glasses. I would tell her: "Just put them on." But what if she couldn't make anything out through the lenses? After all, they fit *my* prescription. So didn't that mean everything would be a blur to her? And—come to think of it—how come they just happened to fit my prescription? Was that just a coincidence? Or had someone meant for me to find them? Had they, in fact, been made specifically for me?

Yeah, right, I told myself. I was becoming a paranoid conspiracy nut.

The end-of-first-period bell rang, and those girls who had phys ed second period started streaming down the stairs. *I* had phys ed second period. I put the glasses on so that I wouldn't get run over, then I kept them on for class because I'm bad enough at volleyball even when I can see. I kept them on even though Tiffanie Mills is in my class.

Coach Roycroft blew his whistle at me and said, "Lose the sunglasses until *after* you win the Olympics, Selmeyer."

Tiffanie, my team's captain, called out, "They're not a fashion statement, Coach. She lost her regular glasses."

"Broke," I corrected, though I was amazed she'd been paying enough attention to know my personal troubles, much less intervene on my behalf. She was probably worried about a delay-of-game penalty. I tried not to look at her, with her warts and wrinkles and all, and her upper arms flapping every time she bounced the ball. At least her gym shorts didn't reveal any more than her skirt had, and I felt personally indebted to whoever it was who'd invented the sports bra.

I was sure the little blue guys would show up—that they always hung around the gym, and that they were the explanation behind my total inability to make actual contact with the ball whenever it came at me. But either they'd gone totally invisible or I simply have no athletic talent at all: No little blue guys, no dead guys, no more guys with pointy ears. The only weird thing was Tiffanie jiggling, wiggling, and flapping all over the court. It was hard to concentrate. Kaylee Shipperd returned a serve right into the side of my head, sending my glasses flying off my face and onto the floor.

Of course, without the glasses, I couldn't see well enough to find the glasses.

But I could make out Tiffanie bending down. "Amazing," she said. I wondered if, holding the glasses, she had caught sight of something dead, blue, or pointed, but then she added, "They didn't break."

By then I'd reached her. "Thanks," I said, trying to lift the frames out of her hand.

But she didn't let go.

"You realize," she told me, "these are the ugliest glasses I have ever seen in my entire life, barring only the goggles Mrs. Spagnola wore after her cataract surgery."

Even though—to my bare eyes—Tiffanie was back to looking straight out of a fashion magazine's pages, I didn't feel she was one to talk about ugly. Still, I didn't say so. "Can I just have them back, please?" I tugged a bit harder—but carefully, not wanting to rip the arm piece off.

Coach Roycroft blew his whistle so that we would hurry up, and Tiffanie, with her wrinkled-nose little smile, released the glasses.

But she glanced down just as she did, and I was close enough to see her startled expression. I was also close enough to see what she saw: her hand, seen through the lenses, gnarled and spotted.

Except by then I had a firm hold on the glasses, and I popped them back onto my nose and around my ears.

Through the lenses, Tiffanie once again looked like the witch out of *Hansel and Gretel*. I saw her claw-like hand extend toward my face, ready to rip the glasses away, and I stepped back, tripping over Merilee Penzak's big feet. I didn't fall, but bobbled backward so that Tiffanie's hand closed on empty air.

She glared at me. I knew she could see her reflection in the mirrored surfaces, but I could only presume her image there looked normal—otherwise she would have noticed back in biology.

Coach Roycroft blew the whistle yet again. "Did we come here to play?" he demanded.

Well, no. Most of us came because it's a state requirement.

Tiffanie backed off.

I went up to the coach and said, "I broke my regular glasses, and these are prescription lenses, but they're making it too dark in here for me to see well enough to play." That was an out-and-out lie, because the tinted lenses did not make the windowless room any dimmer—though they should have.

Coach Roycroft looked skeptical. He'd had me for two years of gym classes and he knew I wasn't an enthusiast. But he jerked his head toward the bleachers, and I sat out the rest of the period.

In the locker room, I made sure I was always in the middle of a cluster of girls so that Tiffanie couldn't corner me.

Which didn't prevent her from smacking me on the back of my head with her geometry book as we all funneled out in the hallway. She tried to make it look like an accident, like she was just waving her book around while simultaneously walking, talking, and looking for her journalism homework paper. I knew she'd been hoping to knock my glasses clear off my face. Luckily her aim wasn't as good as Kaylee's had been. If there hadn't been all those other people around, I suspected Tiffanie would have tackled me and ripped those glasses off.

Third and fourth period, Tiffanie and I had different classes, though I kept alert in the hallways. And, as the morning wore on, I tried to convince myself that whatever was up with the glasses had worn off because everything looked as it should.

But then when I went to the cafeteria for lunch, I saw the tiny blue guys again—pushing the long serving spoons so the handles would fall into the vats of soup and rigatoni, loosening the shaker cap on the bottle of Italian dressing, sitting on the pats of butter— I can only hope simply to melt them with body heat.

And then there was Tiffanie—which did nothing for my appetite, because she still looked like the poster child for Dr. Frankenstein's Nursing Home for the Terminally Ugly. I hung so close to Shelley that when Nancy Jean, Anna, and Lisa—our usual lunch crowd—joined us, Nancy Jean asked, "You two a couple?"

I spotted Julian paying for his lunch. I was all for getting a boy to join our table. Especially a gorgeous boy. Even if he only looked gorgeous through my lenses. I was just raising my arm when Tiffanie flounced up to him.

Look out, I wanted to warn him.

I don't think I'd ever seen the two of them even notice each other before, but now I saw her witchy fingers clutching his sleeve. She stood on tiptoe and he leaned down so she could get closer to his ear.

Tiffanie Mills whispering something to Julian York?

He looked up.

Right at me.

Then, as though that had been coincidence, he continued to glance around the cafeteria, his gaze stopping at the table where he usually sat, like, *Oh, yeah, THERE'S my table.*

Tiffanie drifted away as though she'd never stopped him.

The whole thing couldn't have taken more than five seconds.

My arm fell back to the table. Nancy Jean, who'd started a story about Mrs. Robellard's fourth-period class, was still talking. Nobody seemed to have noticed anything amiss.

They know each other, I thought. *All this year, they've been pretending to be strangers, but as soon as she realizes I can see her as she really looks, she goes to HIM—the one other person who looks different through my glasses.*

I remembered how nice Julian had been outside of Mrs. Starr's office, worrying about a concussion, feeling my head for bumps.

But then I remembered that I'd had the glasses up on top of my head. I remembered our hands knocking against each other as he, helpfully—casually—tried to remove my glasses.

Had his kindness all been a ploy? Had he, too,

realized—before Tiffanie had—that I could see things differently through these glasses?

Had he simply been trying to get them from me?

I realized he and Tiffanie must somehow be in this together. Whatever *this* was.

And I wasn't in this with anyone.

8

School Bus Madness

Earth to Wendy," Nancy Jean said. "Earth calling Wendy."

I turned from gawking at Julian York and saw that my friends had all been watching me watch him.

Shelley told the others, "Wendy has developed a sudden fascination with Julian."

"No, I haven't," I protested. I didn't want Lisa, who can be helpful to the point of being annoying, to decide that it would be a friendly thing to wave Julian over to our table.

But I didn't need Lisa to complicate matters.

"Hi, Julian," Anna said.

Let her be teasing, I hoped.

I turned around, and there he was.

"Hi, everybody," Julian said. "How're you doing, Wendy?"

My friends all wore that *ooo-a-boy* expression that we should have outgrown after first grade.

When, before, had Julian ever approached a tableful of girls and tried to strike up a conversation? Fortunately, we weren't the only ones there: Besides the five of us, five ninth graders had taken over the other half of the table, and they'd unrolled a huge posterboard chart that they were frantically writing on, coloring in, and gluing stuff to, all at a level of frenzy that indicated they needed to have it finished by next period, if not sooner. With their stuff spread out, there was obviously no way for Julian to squeeze in.

Which didn't stop Lisa from glancing around as though searching for a nearby stray chair which she could invite him to pull up. I brought my foot down hard on hers.

"Hi, Julian," I answered, about two beats after all the others had already said hi, and at just about the same time Lisa cried, "Ow!" Then, since he'd asked and might use my not answering as an excuse to hang around, I said, "I'm feeling much better."

Fortunately, though he'd glanced at Lisa at her

outcry, he didn't inquire into the state of her well-being.

I was smiling and nodding like an idiot, but he wasn't moving on. I added, "Thanks." Then, indicating the others, I said, "Support group." What did it take for this guy to catch a hint? "*Girls* support group." I was still smiling like someone without a brain in her head, and nodding like one of those bobble-head dashboard ornaments.

Lisa was scowling and rubbing her foot, and the others—even the ones I wasn't within kicking range of—had caught on not to say anything. They just grinned at Julian, not looking that much more intelligent than me.

"Okay," he finally said. "Good. Well . . . see you."

"See you," we all chanted, except for Lisa, who was still sulking.

He finally carried his tray over to the guys he usually sat with.

"What was that all about?" Shelley asked. "I thought you liked the looks of him."

"I changed my mind," I explained, sounding sharper than I'd intended.

Shelley raised her eyebrows at me.

Nancy Jean said, "He's not bad. We wouldn't make fun of you if you liked him."

Anna said, "Not the way we would if you liked...say..." She paused as though to consider, but finished in a tone of self-satisfied glee: "Nicholas Bonafini!"

"Nicholas Bonafini was *hot* in kindergarten," I protested over their laughter. Anna and Nancy Jean and Lisa had gone to a different elementary school and had never seen him in his prime. I added, "And that's the last time I share *anything* private with any of you."

We were all laughing, even Lisa now that she'd gotten sidetracked from my—as far as she could tell—unwarranted attack on her toes. And I knew they were good and faithful friends and that they would not treat any serious mental disorder on my part as lightly as they would treat a kindergarten crush on a guy who hadn't aged gracefully.

But I couldn't tell them about what I'd been seeing. I couldn't have any of them try on the glasses to see if they worked for everyone, or just me.

Because I was suddenly afraid of Julian York and Tiffanie Mills. They knew I knew their secret. Well, obviously not all of it, but certainly what had to be an important part of it. Having my friends put on those secret-revealing glasses might put them in danger, too.

I might not have the nerve to talk back to a teacher, but I'm not such a coward that I'd endanger my friends.

NEITHER JULIAN nor Tiffanie made any further attempts to talk to me that afternoon. Of course, that could have been because I kept myself surrounded by people.

Or it could have meant, I realized as I got on the bus to go home and noticed Julian—sitting in the back, casually reading a paperback—that they could afford to wait. Julian lived only one street over from me. He knew which was my house.

While I was worrying about that, Tiffanie—who normally rides a different bus—got on ours, in all her wrinkled, sagging, spotted croniness. "I have a note from my mother," she said, waving a sheet of paper at the driver. "I'm supposed to go to my aunt's house, so you can drop me off on the corner of Highland Avenue and Meadowbrook."

Oh, what a coincidence: Julian's stop. And how far is that, again, from where I live? Oh yeah. One block away.

Check the handwriting! I wanted to scream at the driver. *Her mother never wrote that!*

Then I thought, *Her mother?* And I wondered

what kind of mother does a hundred-year-old crone have?

That thought was so bad, I had to look at her over the tops of my glasses.

The driver, who'd no doubt lost a good deal of his morning giving the police his accident report, wasn't in the mood for chatting. He didn't even glance at the note and waved her on.

Tiffanie greeted various friends as she walked down the aisle. "Hey, Lilly. How's it going, Hannah? Hiya, Wendy. I didn't know you rode this bus."

Yeah, right.

And because Shelley was staying after school—Wednesdays she works on the school paper—there was an empty seat next to me. Tiffanie plunked herself down, flashing a big, yellow-toothed grin.

They were going to follow me home, I knew it. To do what? I had no idea—I just knew that these two had something to hide, and I didn't want to find out how desperate they were to keep their true appearances secret. And I wouldn't even have the theoretical help of my wicked stepsister to protect me because she was meeting Mom at the nursing home.

Except that *that* thought was a help.

"Stop!" I shouted as the bus driver closed the doors and started to pull out of his parking space.

We'd traveled about two feet, and he slammed on the brake so hard, I had no doubt that he'd mentally flashed back to the scene this morning: the car striking down the woman in the crosswalk.

I scrambled to my feet and over Tiffanie, who couldn't very well tackle me in front of about forty witnesses. I was talking as I made my way to the front of the bus: "I forgot. I'm supposed to get on bus seventy-four ninety to go to the nursing home to visit my grandmother."

From his expression, I'm pretty sure the driver was considering telling me, *Tough luck.*

I said, "She's not doing well."

Which was true enough, but then she hadn't been doing well for the last year.

I couldn't believe I was announcing personal stuff for the entire busload of kids to hear.

The driver said, "Then you should have gone directly to bus seventy-four ninety."

"Sorry," I said. Maybe my real desperation made me sound pathetic. Maybe he was so relieved that he hadn't been about to run someone over that he figured nothing else was important. He put the bus in PARK and opened the doors. "Cross the parking lot carefully," he said, the emphasis making his tone more hostile than the words should have sounded.

"Thank you," I said. I went down the stairs, and heard the hiss as the doors closed behind me. I was pretty sure neither Tiffanie nor Julian had followed. What could they do? Tiffanie admit that her note was forged? Julian claim that he, too, was supposed to visit an elderly relative, though he had no long-standing dispensation from the office?

But I turned just to make sure.

Only me out there on the pavement.

I waved at my driver, who jerked his thumb backward down the line of buses that were waiting for him before they could go anywhere. So that I wouldn't be walking while buses were moving, he didn't start until I'd reached number 7490, the fifth bus in line, and tapped on the door for that driver to open up and let me in.

"Having trouble making your mind up?" 7490's driver asked.

I figured she didn't really want an answer, so I simply started down the aisle.

"Hey!" the driver called. "I need a note."

Why do some adults feel they have to treat us like we're little kids trying to get away with something?

Not, of course, that I *wasn't* trying to get away with something. But still...

"There's a standing order for me to be able to

visit my grandmother at Westfall Nursing Home," I said.

The driver looked at me as though I was asking her for money.

"I've been on this bus before." When was the last time? April? No, it had to be before spring break.

From a quarter of the way down the aisle, Gia called, "She's my sister. There's a note for both of us on file in the office." Pretty helpful, for a wicked stepsister.

Maybe the driver remembered that I, too, did occasionally ride this bus, though not as regularly as Gia, or maybe she just didn't really care and had only been giving me a hard time out of force of habit. In any case she said, "Find a seat," and almost simultaneously closed the door and pulled out into traffic.

I staggered down the aisle, holding on to the backs of seats to keep from ending up in anyone's lap.

"Thanks," I muttered as I passed Gia.

She was sitting next to Kaylee Shipperd, the two of them with their heads bent over a teen magazine survey. Gia grunted at me, but didn't ask why I'd changed my mind about visiting Nana. Kaylee never looked up.

The only empty seat was way in the back of the bus, next to this big, ugly upperclassman who'd taken off his shoes and was sitting sideways with his bare feet on the seat.

"Do you mind?" I had to ask.

He sighed loudly before taking his feet down, leaving sweaty little prints behind. And he never did put his shoes back on.

9

Escape to the Nursing Home

Gia and I got off the bus at Westfall Nursing Home, and I would have defied anybody watching us to guess we knew each other.

The day being so nice, we encountered various old folk making their way—mostly via wheelchair, walker, or cane—round the drive and the paths of the front garden, or sitting on the front porch. There was a backyard enclosed by a high brick wall for those residents who needed supervision, those who were more easily confused and apt to wander off and not remember how to get back.

In theory, Nana was a backyard resident, though in truth she didn't have much interest in going outside, much less wandering off, regardless of the weather. It was hard to tell *what* she was interested in since she'd pretty much stopped talking back before Christmas. Still, a few of the aides would periodically plunk her down in a wheelchair and take her for a spin around the grounds.

One or two of the residents on the porch looked familiar and some nodded or said hello as we approached. One of the ladies called out, "Hello, Gia. Brought your little sister today?" even though I am only two and a half months younger, which—statistically speaking—doesn't count as younger at all.

Gia took the opportunity to make herself at home with them, chatting, adjusting lap blankets—old people love their lap blankets, even come August—examining and exclaiming over a scarf one of them was knitting, studying a Scrabble board and providing one of the players with a twenty-seven-point word. (*Demure*. What kind of fifteen-year-old thinks up the word *demure*?)

My feeling was that old people are kind of spooky—I mean you can hardly tell what some of them are saying because they've had strokes or they don't have their teeth. And they ask you questions, and you have no idea what they're talking about, and they tell *you* to speak up, speak clearly, stop mumbling.

But Gia, with her plans to go into geriatric medicine, knew what to say to them. And they loved her for it. She promised that if she was still around when *Wheel of Fortune* came on, she'd sit in the lobby with them and watch.

I, meanwhile, just stood there and smiled a lot, while they sat there and thought Gia had an idiot for a sister.

What if, I worried, *my glasses make me see something I don't want to see?* If ever there was a place that was going to be haunted, it would be a nursing home. If someone started talking to me, I'd have to make sure he was really there before I answered. Some of them looked nearly as old as Tiffanie, but they did whether I looked at them through the lenses or over.

Finally Gia told the people on the porch she was going in to see "our" grandmother. (*Not YOUR grandmother,* I thought, though she probably just figured that was easier than explaining.)

"She's a lucky woman to have two such beautiful and attentive granddaughters," one of the women said.

Yeah, lucky. She didn't even recognize us anymore.

And Gia was both the beautiful and the attentive one.

Nana's room is on the fifth floor, and that's where we found her. She was sitting up in a chair that faced the window, which looked out over the north end of Highland Park across the street, where the lilacs were in full bloom. Her expression appeared alert and intent. But I'd been here other times when she wore the same expression facing the wall.

Her roommate turned her head, though, and her eyes above the oxygen mask followed us.

"Hello, Mrs. Rausch," I said, proud of myself for remembering her name, but thinking, *Wow, she's lost so much weight I wouldn't recognize her.*

Gia looked at me in horror and whispered, "That's not Mrs. Rausch. Mrs. Rausch died two weeks ago. This is why polite people don't wear sunglasses indoors." She raised her voice above the hiss of the oxygen tank: "Hello, Miss Lysiak."

The figure on the bed gave a feeble wave.

I was just glad the glasses didn't show Mrs. Rausch still lingering in the room.

Gia took Miss Lysiak's hand, thin as a bird's foot and bruised from IV needles, and leaned over to kiss her cheek. She knew this woman for less than two weeks, and already she felt comfortable kissing her.

I moved in to Nana's section of the room. "Hi, Nana," I said.

No reaction.

Self-consciously, I bent over to kiss her cheek, which was dry and papery.

Still no reaction.

For about five seconds.

Then she raised her hand to touch where my lips had grazed her. But she never glanced my way.

Wake up, Nana, I wanted to shout, though she was awake. *Snap out of it.*

I remembered a time when I'd been four or five, when she'd come running out to the car to greet us on a Sunday visit, me, my mother, and my dad, and she picked me up, tickled my neck with a multitude of extravagant kisses, then twirled me round and round and round until, dizzy, laughing, we'd fallen on our backs onto her front lawn. Then it felt as though we remained still, lying in the fragrant, fresh-mowed grass, while everthing else—the house, the front yard, the apple tree that Papa had planted to celebrate their first wedding anniversary—spun around us.

I threw myself into the armchair and wondered if I should turn on the TV. But Nana was so clearly not interested that it would be obvious I had turned it on for myself.

While Gia talked quietly with Miss Lysiak, I let my gaze wander around the room. On the dresser was Mom and Bill's wedding picture, the two of them looking radiant, flanked by me and Gia, ten years old and sulky about each other and about the uncomfortable and fussy bridesmaid dresses we'd been forced to wear. I remember we'd squabbled right before the photographer called us up onto the altar to take our picture. Gia had recovered her poise and you'd have to know her to know she was mad. Me...Well, if I'd realized I'd have this picture to look at for the rest of my life, maybe I could have mustered a more agreeable expression.

There were other pictures stuck in the frame of the dresser mirror and scattered around the room, and also a photo album on the nightstand. I knew that periodically Mom would rearrange the pictures, and exchange a new album for the old one. At first, when Nana had been better, the two of them used to look through the albums together, but the last year it had been pretty clear, even to Mom, that Nana wasn't seeing the pictures anymore. Maybe Mom still brought the albums so that the aides, some of whom changed about as often as the seasons, could glimpse what she'd been like before.

I dragged the photo album over onto my lap. It was one of the older ones, with pictures of Nana's parents and her sister, who'd died of polio when she'd been about my age, and a whole bunch of people I didn't know. I flipped to the back where her wedding pictures were. I didn't remember Papa at all; he'd died before I was a year old. I only knew him through Nana's stories. And Nana's stories about Papa had been one of the last things that left her. When my parents were still married, Nana had been fine: living on her own, taking care of the house and yard, organizing the women's guild at her church, visiting as Story Lady at the local library. It was after the divorce, actually after Mom married Bill, that there were the first signs of trouble: Nana kept calling Bill "Eugene." *I* thought it was funny. I thought she was hinting that she didn't like Mom's new husband, and that was why she called him by my father's name. I wasn't even worried when Nana called me by my Mom's name, Jeannette. Nana would roll her eyes, smack herself on the forehead, and correct herself by saying "Wendy." Until the day when she didn't catch on that she'd used the wrong name. Until the day she wouldn't believe me when I said that I wasn't Jeannette.

It had all started when Bill and Gia came into our lives. Thinking about it, I knew that was coincidence; but feelings don't necessarily make sense, and they can be stubborn. It was hard—when I was having a bad day about something or other—not to wonder.

Gia finally finished with Miss Lysiak and came and gave Nana a hug and a kiss. "How are you feeling, Nana?" she asked, giving her a quick little shoulder massage.

No reaction to Gia, either, which was petty of me to gloat over.

Gia kept on. "What a pretty sweater you're wearing. I love the embroidery. Is it one of the ones you made? Wow, look at those tiny stitches, Wendy."

It *was* one of the ones she'd made. She'd made me one just like it with the tiny blue forget-me-nots along the bottom border. But mine had been made to fit an eight-year-old, and it was given away to the Salvation Army so that another little girl could enjoy it. I wondered if yet another child had it now, or if it was at the bottom of someone's closet, or if it had been thrown away.

Gia plunked herself on the edge of Nana's bed and lifted the photo album away from me. "Oh, I love this album," she said. "This is the one where you were growing up. Here, let's look at it together." She was positioned between the two of us, but Nana continued to look out the window, and I leaned back and stared at the ceiling.

As Gia chattered away about the pictures, I wanted to tell her: *She's not like the others. You can't charm her. Not only does she not know who we are, she isn't even aware we're here. You can be as personable as you want, and she won't care.* That gave me a certain amount of satisfaction—to know that Nana couldn't be comparing the two of us and liking Gia better.

Gia said, "Oh, and here you are in that blue and white dress that was handmade for you in Italy. We still have that, you know, and a couple other of your special dresses, like your Japanese kimono, and the green suit you wore when you and Papa got married. Look at all these handsome young men you knew. I bet they were all courting you."

Courting. I sniffed. That fit along with *demure.*

Still, I glanced at the page Gia was looking at, where Nana was a young woman, surrounded by friends, all laughing and having a good time.

How many of them were dead now? Were any in the same state as Nana? Probably not. Nana was lucky enough to be suffering from *early* Alzheimer's. Like regular Alzheimer's wasn't bad enough.

I was feeling claustrophobic and I stood up.

Gia seemed as oblivious to me as Nana was.

When will Mom get here? I wondered. *And how much should I tell her about what's been going on?* She wasn't likely to let me transfer to a different school starting tomorrow without *some* sort of explanation.

If I didn't have the glasses tomorrow, if I told Tiffanie and Julian that I'd thrown them away because they gave me a headache and made everything look blurry so I could hardly see anything, would they believe me? And leave me alone?

On the other hand, what would they do to me if they didn't believe me?

"I need to go for a walk," I announced.

No one was interested.

I went back down to the main floor and was trying to decide whether I should go into the back garden or out onto South Avenue when I saw, through the glass door, Julian coming up the front walk.

10

Escape to the Garden

I froze like a deer startled by headlights. But I
snapped out of that when I thought of what
happens to deer that don't move out of the way
of traffic.

I had to do something—but what?

I could scream for help, and—when the aides or
nurses came—explain that Julian was stalking me.

Which he would deny, of course.

But I could always tell *why* he was stalking me. I
could demand, "Look at him through these glasses."

Except for that nagging worry that nobody else
would see what I saw.

He'd paused just on the other side of the door,

talking with—or being talked to by—the residents on the porch. With the sunlight outside glaring on the glass, I was pretty sure he hadn't seen me yet.

I could run for the elevator, but if it had been called to a different floor, I'd be stranded there waiting in the wide open when he came in. And even if the elevator came, what then? Go upstairs to Nana's room? Did he know her name? I realized he didn't need to know it. *Two girls come here,* he could say, and either describe us or give our names. *And who do they visit?* he'd ask. Gia's fan club would assume he was in love with her, just as they were, and they would think that was sweet, and they would tell him, *Oh, that's Helen Vogt's granddaughter you're looking for, up in room five fifteen.*

There was no reason for Julian to harm Nana or Gia, so if I ran, it wasn't like I was abandoning them. But run where?

I could zip into one of the resident's rooms on this floor to hide. And hope there was nobody in the room who was susceptible to heart attacks or who would scream at my sudden entrance.

You're being ridiculous, I told myself. What could Julian do to me here?

But there was a good chance, with those pointy ears and fickle facial features, that he wasn't human.

There was, in truth, no telling *what* he could do. And if one of the residents later said, *A hysterical girl came into my room, then a young man followed her and chopped her into little pieces and flushed her down my toilet,* was anybody going to believe a nursing home patient? They'd give her an aspirin and extra Jell-O for dinner and tell her to watch *Wheel of Fortune* from now on, and not the SciFi Channel.

Was the library any better? If, for any reason, he chose to go there, I would be trapped, for there was only the one entrance.

Kitchen? Too far down the hallway, given that the front door was already moving as Julian pushed on it to come in.

I turned and dashed for the side exit, the one that opened into the backyard. I knew it was enclosed, but—after all—that wall was meant to contain geriatric patients, not fleeing-for-their-lives fifteen-year-olds. At the very least, it was a half acre with trees and bushes and a little windy path that had park benches every ten feet or so, which would afford some amount of cover. And if I was really lucky, Julian would be concentrating on finding the elevator and wouldn't even see me leave the building.

"Wendy!" I heard him call.

So much for luck.

I hit the door and almost bowled over an aide assisting a man with a walker. "Hey! Slow down!" she yelled after me.

"Sorry," I called over my shoulder as I kept on running.

Ignoring the path, I ran straight: onto the grass, into a cluster of trees. There really weren't as many as I had hoped. Which made sense if you remembered the whole purpose was to air the patients without losing them.

So I veered for the wall, thinking I could scramble over and—I hoped—lose him in the neighborhood.

"Hey!" I heard the aide yell a second time. "No running, you two!"

Julian was too close behind me. If I didn't make it over that wall on the first try, he'd be right on top of me. And if the wall was that easy for me to just fly over, it wouldn't slow him down, either.

And what street was on the other side of that wall, anyway? Already I was disoriented. If I came out on South, which was a busy street, somebody was sure to notice if Julian...what? Pulled a knife on me? Cast a spell on me? Dragged me into a nearby spaceship? And just because people were driving by, that didn't mean any of them could stop, or would even *try to* stop in time to rescue me—even assuming they could tell I needed rescuing and that we weren't just horsing around. Robinson might be a good street to come out on, being residential, but what if it was Mount Hope Avenue on the other side of the wall—which was lined with mostly empty parking lots?

I could dodge behind one of the trees and hope that Julian went right past, without circling around it and coming face-to-face with me.

I glanced over my shoulder.

He was gaining.

There was another little stand of trees, and I ran into that, and out the other side a moment later, around the gazebo, headed for some more trees, saw an archway—and lost track of where I was.

Oh, yeah, I thought, *those arches the lilac committee put up.* I knew it wasn't the one near my house, all the way across the park, but assumed they must have put up a bunch of them, never mind that Highland Park was across the street, not on Westfall Nursing Home grounds.

I sped through the arch—which sure looked like granite, though I knew it couldn't be—and there were a lot more trees on the far side, for which I was grateful. I zigzagged, watching the ground so I wouldn't trip over tree roots, and wondered if now was the time to try hiding. I couldn't hear Julian anymore, so I glanced over my shoulder.

Not a sign of him.

Of course, not a sign of the arch, either.

Or the wall.

Or the nursing home.

And there were *a lot* of trees.

A whole lot.

Even when I looked over the tops of my lenses.

I was in a forest. Not a wooded yard. Not a park.

A freaking forest.

11

The More I Escape,
the Deeper Trouble I Get Into

There was no time to panic. I heard Julian call, "Wendy!" His voice was close by. I was pretty sure it came from the direction I was facing, from where the gate, and—beyond that—Westfall Nursing Home should be, and wasn't.

On the other hand, I heard the crackling of brush coming from the other way, the direction in which I had been heading.

It was probably a case of sound echoing or bouncing off all those tree trunks, but I *had* been zigzagging, and I was willing to grant that finding myself in a forest in the middle of what should have been a backyard might have disoriented me.

Might have.

He *was* closing in. I just wasn't sure from which direction.

So I dived off to the side, behind a fallen tree, into a patch of really tall wildflowers, thinking only at the last moment that I would be lucky not to impale myself on any of the branches.

Twigs jabbed me, but didn't inflict any fatal injuries—or at least not immediately fatal injuries. I raised my head from my prone position and peeked over the tree trunk. I saw that, for all my elusive maneuvering since going through the gate, I'd been following a path that ribboned through the trees.

And standing on that path, not five feet away, having caught up some time between my last glance in that direction and now, was Julian. The path was so twisty, there was a chance he hadn't seen my graceful hurtle into the vegetation even though he appeared to be looking directly at me. I told myself this was probably an optical illusion. I didn't duck, lest that movement attract his attention.

My heart was beating so fast and loud, I wasn't aware of any other sound. So I was taken completely by surprise when five men burst onto the scene, no doubt the brush cracklers from the other end of the path. Like Julian, they were tall, slender, and pointyearred. But there the similarity ended, for instead of jeans and T-shirts, they wore clothes right out of a Renaissance festival—tunics over breeches and tall boots—and they carried weapons: bows and swords and daggers.

Julian must have called in reinforcements, I realized. I didn't stand a chance.

But they sure looked startled to come face-to-face with one another: Julian, who had been preoccupied with pursuing me, and the men, who'd been making so much noise that they wouldn't have been able to hear much beyond themselves.

Four of the men went for their swords—not the kind of move people who are working together generally make. The one who had not unsheathed his sword told the others, "Don't kill him unless you absolutely have to." Definitely on the wrong side of friendly.

So much for my ability to assess a situation.

Julian dodged one of the two guys who lunged at him, but the second tackled him, and both of them went sprawling in the dirt. While the man who had given the don't-kill-him order stood aside, all four of the others kicked and pummeled Julian until he stopped struggling. I'd seen guys horsing around before—I'd even seen sports brawls—but this went beyond that into vicious. Then they dragged him up on his knees, bruised and bloody, and one of them, Mr. Don't-Kill-Him—the leader?—placed a sword blade to Julian's throat.

"Well met, Julwin Y'orick," that one said. "This will give us some bargaining power."

Julian looked mad enough to spit, only his good manners holding him back. "My father will not deal with you just because you hold me hostage," he snapped.

"Then your father will get you back one piece at a time, and he can reassemble you to bury you," said the other man.

Man. Who was I kidding? These were no men.

He was an elf.

They were all elves.

I peeked over the top of my glasses to see what these guys would look like in normal vision and got two surprises:

(1) They still looked the same. Even Julian. In this place I'd accidentally found, whatever it was that caused Julian to pass for normal no longer worked.

(2) Either wearing these glasses all day had cured my nearsightedness, or being in this place—wherever this place was—had. Because despite the distance, I could see clearly.

Just when I thought I'd caught on to the way things worked.

That old saying, "The enemy of my enemy is my friend," came to mind, and I considered whether I should announce myself to Julian's attackers. But Julian wasn't exactly an enemy. And would these guys be any happier than he was to know I could see them and had wandered into their world? What made me think that five punks who would beat up on a single, unarmed guy would treat me any better?

I waited for Julian's attackers to notice me, for them to come over and chop my head off since I didn't make a good hostage, my father being in Hong Kong, my mother being in Syracuse, and my mother's current husband being in an all-day performance appraisal meeting. And, in any case, I guessed none of them was likely to have anything this group of bully warrior elves would want.

Or—just in case they didn't notice me on their own—there was the possibility that Julian would tell them, "Hey, you want someone who doesn't belong here? Try behind that tree trunk over there."

But he didn't.

Of course, there was no reason to believe they would treat him any better if he turned me over to them, so that was no reason for me to go and feel grateful to him or anything.

But I was seriously spooked by those guys and the rough way they handled Julian as they bound his hands behind his back and taunted him with threats of violence whether or not his father gave in to their demands—whatever *they* were. So I was...okay, I'll admit to *relieved*. I was relieved Julian didn't give away my hiding spot.

Don't look this way, I mentally begged the elves. If they took Julian away, I could head back the way I'd come, find that gateway back into my own world....

I ignored the little voice that reminded me I hadn't gone that far beyond the arch before glancing back. Sure, I'd zigged, I'd even zagged, but I still should have been able to see the arch.

What if it was a one-way passage? What if I couldn't get back home, but was stuck here where the natives were less than cordial and I'd let the only person I knew get taken away by thugs intent on putting him through the elven equivalent of a food processor?

I am not a very nice person to be worried only about my own skin, the voice of my conscience chimed in.

Hey, it's my skin, I reminded my conscience, *and it's the only skin I've got.*

Besides, what could I do?

Besides, I had no idea what was going on in this

world, who these guys were, or what their grievance was with Julian and his father.

Besides, hadn't I already decided that Julian and Tiffanie were the bad guys?

But I knew I was weaseling: I was too afraid to get involved. I stayed under cover of the fallen tree and the wildflowers, and tried not think about how the leaves and grass were making my skin itch, tried not to breathe, tried not to sweat. My cover, such as it was, was skimpy. Julian had seen me right away, I was sure of it. The only reason these guys hadn't was that they hadn't known about me to begin with. Trying to bolt or sneak away would only attract their attention. I just had to remain motionless and wait them out.

Finally, with Julian bound and helpless, his captors put away their swords.

But when the leader slammed his blade into its sheath, the buckle on his sword belt slipped open, and sword, sheath, and belt ended up around the guy's feet.

Someone started laughing.

I knew right away it wasn't the other elves; they just didn't look like the kind to find the humor in a situation like that. I figured it wasn't Julian because he'd pretty much had the breath kicked out of him.

Besides, the laughter was coming from near me.

Good grief, it wasn't me, was it, getting hysterical or going crazy or something? I didn't think so because the laughter was very high-pitched, more so even than a child's, like a tape on fast-forward, or like someone who'd been inhaling helium.

I tipped my head, slowly so as not to rustle the leaves, and spotted a chipmunk-sized little blue guy on a branch one tree over from me. He was doubled over, holding his stomach, and wheezing from laughing so hard.

"Look at you!" he taunted, his words coming out between the peals of laughter. "Lucky for you I loosened your weapons belt and not the belt to your pants."

The elf took a step toward the little blue guy. But he'd lost track of why he was so angry, and the fallen belt tripped him so that he went sprawling.

The blue guy found this hilarious. He laughed until he sounded about to throw up from laughing so hard. He couldn't get out any more than "You... you...you..." He fell to his knees on the branch, then flopped over onto his back, clutching his stomach and rolling, while the elf tried to kick himself free of the belt around his ankles.

But one of the other elves moved in. He came so

close to where I was lying on my stomach that he stepped on the little finger of my right hand.

Don't scream, don't scream, do NOT scream, I ordered myself, and thought I'd burst from the effort of not even drawing my hand back. Who'd have guessed a skinny elf could weigh so much?

The elf didn't notice what he'd stepped on; he was all focused on the blue guy who was ridiculing his leader. He caught the blue guy up in his hand, evidently taking the blue guy totally by surprise. Evaporated his laughter, that was for sure. "Want me to pop its little head off?" the elf asked, his thumb at the ready under the blue guy's chin, as though he was talking about a dandelion.

The leader motioned for him to come closer.

I curled my fingers into a fist, and only the barest edge of the elf's boot grazed the outside edge of my hand.

The elf leader pointed to another tree that had a little hollow in its trunk. "This'll be slower. Give it time to regret mocking its betters." He bent to pick up a rock from the path.

"No," the little guy begged. "I already regret my foolishness, kind sirs. Kind *better* sirs. What a stupid thing to do. I'm a stupid, worthless creature. I'm sorry to have inflicted myself on you."

They didn't heed him. The one shoved him into the hole, and the other jammed the rock in after him.

"Don't leave me here!" screamed the blue guy, his voice muffled and faint. "I'm sorry, I'm sorry, I'm sorry!"

The elf leader picked up another rock and used that to hammer the first rock deeper into the tree trunk.

There was a bloodcurdling scream. Then silence.

The elf said, "Oops."

"There was no call for that," Julian hissed at them from between clenched teeth.

One of the others kicked him in the small of his back.

Annoying as those blue guys could be, I agreed with Julian. If this elf lived in my world, he'd be the kind of person who swerves his car to hit the raccoon trying to cross the street. I felt my eyes grow hot from the unfairness of bullies.

They'll do the same, more or less, to Julian, that damn conscience of mine warned.

Or to me, I warned my conscience back.

I stayed safely where I was while the elves forced Julian down the path. I stayed, even when—for the briefest instant—his gaze rested on where I lay, and he said nothing.

When I was sure they were gone, I finally allowed myself to stretch out, to lay my head against the coolness of the grass. But I didn't give myself long. No telling if an even worse group of elves would come by.

I glanced apprehensively at the tree where the unfortunate blue guy had met his end. He had to be dead. Didn't he? My mind played with the idea that he might just be injured. Horribly, shockingly injured. There really wasn't anything I could do.

Sure, my conscience jeered at me. *Just like you couldn't do anything for Julian.*

"Oh, shut up," I muttered to myself, thinking the emphasis of actually speaking out loud might help convince me. This might be how those demented street people started: overactive consciences.

My stomach churning queasily, I set my hand on the rock that was jutting out of the tree trunk. I prepared myself to avert my eyes at the first hint of blood splatter or gore. I yanked the rock out of the tree trunk and squeamishly glanced into the opening. Then a second glance. Then a longer third glance. Then I just went ahead and looked.

There was nothing in the hole.

I leaned in closer. There was no opening deeper in the tree that he could have been forced down into. I glanced at the rock, still in my hand.

The little blue guy was clinging to it. Not injured at all. More like a leprechaun hugging the Blarney stone. He puckered his lips in my direction and gave a noisy kiss. "Thanks, sweetie. That saved me a lot of digging." He held up a teeny-tiny spoon that could absolutely never have made even a dent in wood.

But that wasn't my first thought. My first thought was: *Eek!*

I dropped the rock.

Fortunately for him, the blue guy let go, so when the rock landed, it didn't land on him. "Hey!" he complained, standing on the ground, hands on hips accusingly.

"Sorry," I said. "I thought you were dead."

"Oh." He threw himself onto his back. "Were you ready to give me mouth-to-mouth?"

"Yuck," I said. "Absolutely not. Don't be disgusting."

He flung his arm across his forehead, like a silent screen actress about to swoon. "I'm failing fast!" he proclaimed. "Get those big, luscious lips over here."

"I do not have big lips," I protested. I couldn't even bring myself to say *luscious.*

"Hey, they're big from where I stand," the blue guy said, even though, technically, he was lying down. He squeezed his eyes shut and pursed his own itty-bitty lips.

NOW YOU SEE IT...

"Nice meeting you," I lied. "Glad to see you aren't dead." Well, I *had been*—until he started talking. "Good-bye." I stepped around him and onto the path, because—as he was so icky—there was no way I was going to step *over* him, even though I was wearing jeans and not a skirt he could look up.

"Hey!" he called after me. "Hey!"

I ignored him as I started back the way I'd come, but the next thing I knew, I felt him land on my shoulder. How could he do that? From the ground to almost five feet straight up into the air when he was no taller than—you'll excuse the expression—my extended middle finger?

"Hey!" he shouted into my ear.

I brushed him off like dandruff.

A moment later he was on my other shoulder.

"Hey!" he shouted into that ear.

"Get off me," I demanded, never stopping. "I do not allow"—what the heck was he, anyway?—"little...blue...*whatevers* to take a free ride on my body."

He made a throaty growl like a cat in heat. "Sounds sexy," he said.

I swatted him off again.

This time I saw tiny iridescent wings unfurl from between the folds of his shirt. Well, I didn't so much *see* them as *extrapolate* that's what must have happened, because he was hovering in front of my face like a nervy hummingbird, those wings moving in a blur as he flew backward to keep up with me.

"Spreenie," he said.

"Excuse me?"

"I'm a spreenie."

All right, he had my curiosity going for him. Though I refused to slow down. "What's a spreenie?"

In a voice that was no doubt meant to mimic me, though he didn't sound a bit like me, he said, "It's a...little...blue...*whatever.*"

"Wonderful," I said. "Thank you so much for completing my education."

"Larry," he said.

"What?"

"My name is Larry."

I stopped. He did, too. "What kind of name is Larry..." I realized I couldn't finish with "for a spreenie" since he was the first one I was being introduced to. But still. You'd figure in a magical world...

I started walking again, and he started flying backward again to keep that eight or ten inches from my face.

"And you're a human," he said. "See, I know more than you do. And your name is...?"

I knew it probably wasn't a good idea, but I told him, "Wendy."

"So where are we going, Wendy?"

"*We* are not going anywhere," I informed him. "*I* am going back home." I did not add, *I hope.*

"Well," he said, "unless you came through another portal besides the nearest one, you've passed it."

"No," I told him. "Even though you've been a distracting little nuisance, I would have seen the archway if I'd passed it."

Larry laughed so hard he did a backward somersault. "Silly Wendy," he said, once he caught his breath. "You're going the wrong way."

"This is the way I came," I said.

"But you can't see it going from east to west," he said, "only from west to east."

I ignored him.

"Check," he urged me, pointing behind me.

He was only trying to trick me into proving myself a gullible fool.

But I knew I'd already traveled farther than I had coming in. So I turned around.

And there, right in the middle of the path where I'd just walked through, impossible to miss—except, of course, that I'd missed it—was the archway.

And even though—whether or not I'd seen it—I'd just walked through it, I was *not* back in my own world.

12

Magic Lesson

Than wasn't there a minute ago," I said.

"Of course it was," Larry told me. "You just couldn't see it."

Couldn't see it? The archway was like ten feet tall and ten feet wide, and made of granite. Even without my glasses, I would have had a hard time missing it.

Despite the fact that it sent chills up my back and made my toes curl with anxiety, I went back and touched the thing. The stone was cool and rough. It didn't look weathered at all, so it was probably new. But it was solid enough that it wasn't likely thirty-seconds-new.

Could I really not have seen it coming from the other direction? It wasn't like the path was crowded by an overabundance of trees that could have obscured anything that big, so I walked around the outside of the arch, even though I had to step off the path to do so, to the other side.

As soon as I passed it, the arch disappeared.

Not obscured by trees or by a bend in the path: just...disappeared.

I stepped back, and the arch reappeared.

Though I knew there was the danger of someone coming upon me as I wasted time trying to understand what I suspected was un-understandable, I spent precious moments in the grass and leaned from side to side without moving my feet: As I leaned to the right, the arch would be there one instant, gone the next; when I leaned in the opposite direction, it would come back. I couldn't go slowly enough to see any shrinking or fading: just there, or not there. I pushed the glasses down my nose and looked over the tops. The arch misbehaved no matter how I looked at it. I put both hands on the side of the arch—or at least I tried to: My left hand could touch the solidness of the stone; my right hand felt nothing and passed right through, smacking against my left palm.

Something hit the back of my head. I whirled around just in time to see Larry, standing on a nearby tree branch, hide his hands behind his back.

"Don't you dare throw stones at me," I said, sounding as grumpy as our neighbor Mrs. Freelander, complaining if a kid stepped one foot off the sidewalk onto her lawn.

"I never did," he protested.

"Let me see your hands."

He hesitated, then brought his hands around to the front, empty palms upward—never mind that something bounced off the branch on which he was standing, then dropped to the ground behind him.

"I saw that," I told him.

"It wasn't a stone," he assured me.

Stone, acorn—I wasn't going to quibble.

"Why can I only see the arch from this side?" I asked him.

"Because it's here"—he gestured with his left hand—"but it's not there." He wiggled the fingers of his right hand.

"West to east," I said, repeating what he'd said earlier. "Not east to west."

"Yes," he said with that extra brightness you'd use with a kindergartner who'd finally learned to tie her shoes after making you watch thirty-two failed attempts.

I remembered having seen a similar arch in Highland Park. "Do they all face the same direction?"

Larry gave a dismissive snort. "That would be just plain silly."

How ridiculous of me to even ask.

A sudden, awful idea hit me. "So does that mean I can only travel in one direction? I can't go back to where I was?" It wasn't like I could see the nursing home's garden through the arch—just the stupid path in this stupider forest.

Larry sighed as though I was a real burden. "Of course you can go back."

I had the feeling that, despite his blue color, Larry had the potential to be a lawyer. And I don't mean that in a nice way. I'm thinking about the kind of lawyer who invented the word *loophole*. So I asked, "How does the gate work?"

Larry snorted again. "How does a computer work?" he countered.

"The gate is computerized?" I asked.

He smacked himself on the forehead and said, "No."

"Ah," I said. "You were being sarcastic. You were saying I wouldn't understand—"

Larry looked very pleased with himself.

I finished, "—even *if* you knew."

He had to work that out before he realized I'd insulted him.

Meanwhile, I said, "I don't mean: What is its energy source and what are the physics of its operation? I mean: How do I use it to get home?"

"It transports you where you want to go," Larry said. "But you can't go home." I must have looked ready to go for his tiny blue jugular because he hurriedly added, "I mean, you *can,* but what about the son of the elven king? You can't just abandon him. I mean, I presume by how fast you turned up to let me out of the tree that you were close enough to see Berrech and his rebels abduct him."

Okay, I let myself get sidetracked. *"Julian?* Julian who I go to school with? Julian is the son of the elven king?"

"Duh." Larry smacked himself on the forehead again to show he couldn't believe how dense I was.

Wow. So Julian was a prince. Still... "Julian is the one who chased me in here," I explained.

Larry looked at me skeptically. "Why? What did you do?"

"I didn't do anything."

Larry was giving me the same fishy-eyed look

Mrs. Pincelli, the school secretary, gives kids whose teachers have sent them to see the principal.

Kids who often, I had to admit to myself, made that same claim of innocence.

"My life," I said—recognizing, even as I said it, the overly dramatic sound of that—"was in jeopardy."

"That's doubtful." Larry used his sleazy-lawyer voice to show the contempt he had for that thought. "You mean because of those glasses?" He flipped his wrist dismissively.

I looked at him, through the glasses, then over the frames. Absolutely nothing on this side of the gate looked any different through these lenses. So it wasn't like I was reacting to stuff he couldn't see. How did he know there was anything special about them?

"What do you know about these?" I demanded.

Larry tried to look confused and innocent. "What?" he asked.

"Never mind, Little Mr. Anti-Smurf," I told him. "If Julian is in trouble, I'm sorry for it. But I've got enough troubles of my own without getting involved in a coup d'état in the elven world. I wish I could say it's been nice meeting you. But it hasn't."

It transports you where you want to go, Larry had said. Well, I wanted to go home. I stepped through the archway, wondering how long I'd been away, wondering if my mother had gotten to the nursing home yet, wondering if Gia and my grandmother had missed me—well, Gia, anyway—as they looked through the photo album that had pictures of Nana as a young woman.

It transports you where you want to go.

Sure.

I should have stopped to think how I had certainly never wanted to come here.

13

An Unexpected Side Trip

Just as looking at the arch was a case of "now you see it/now you don't," as I walked through the arch, one instant I could see the path ahead of me winding among trees, trees, and more trees—and then I was suddenly on a street corner: So suddenly, in fact, that I was unbalanced and stumbling off the unexpected curb before I could catch myself.

Even as I fell, I knew there was something wrong, more wrong than falling, which was bad enough, since I was falling off the sidewalk and into the street, where there was oncoming traffic.

But that wasn't the worst of it.

I had been expecting to find myself in the yard of

Westfall Nursing Home. Or even back in the room with Nana and Gia, since I'd been thinking specifically of them. Which hadn't been very smart: Nana, who pretty much lived only in her own mind, wouldn't have been unduly alarmed to see me suddenly wink into existence in front of her, but Gia would have been sure to notice in a negative sort of way.

But I wasn't even on South Avenue or Robinson or any street I recognized. As I fell, my face approaching the pavement—slowly enough to notice things in a surreal way, but too fast to do anything to prevent imminent impact—I glimpsed unusual cars. I mean, I'm not an expert on cars or anything—I classify them by color rather than make—but these were all big and rounded in an old-fashioned kind of way that just screamed, "Wrong! Wrong! Wrong!"

Yet another wrong thing was the people I caught sight of on my way down. A man in an ugly tweed suit, wearing a hat and carrying a big satchel, turned from the doorbell he was about to ring and gawked at me. And there were several women—all dressed in pastel dresses that were buttoned and formfitting on the top, with really full skirts that came below their knees, not a pair of pants or shorts among them. The women, too, wore hats—not like sun hats or rain hats or winter hats, but these itty-bitty why-bother?

hats with flocked netting coming over their fore-heads—giving the impression they all had really nasty collections of freckles, warts, and birthmarks. One of the women had a little girl with her, also wearing a hat, and—as she watched my endless fall—the mother grabbed hold of her child and spun her around to protect her from seeing me flattened and/or splattered. Woman and girl were both wear-ing little white gloves.

Then—finally—I hit the ground, breaking my fall somewhat with my knees and my outstretched palms, though my elbows buckled and my chest hit the ground so hard I was sure my boobs—such as they are—must now be sticking out of my back. Fortunately my face did not make contact with the asphalt, though my glasses went flying.

That was where *fortunately* ended.

I heard the screeching of tires and the blaring of a horn. I could smell the rubber of someone's tires being left behind on the road. Even with my bare eyes, I could see one of those huge cars heading right at me—not straight on but sideways, because the driver, trying desperately to stop, had lost control of his vehicle. Not that sideways versus head-on was going to make much of a difference to me, not at the speed he was going.

Someone grabbed hold of the back of my shirt and yanked.

My collar bit into my throat as my torso was lifted enough off the road so that I flipped onto my back, my knees bent under me.

The car slid through the space I had just been occupying, close enough that I could see its whitewalled tires before the wind, and road grit of its passing made me blink my eyes.

When I opened them again, the car was just resuming normal forward motion rather than its previous slantwise slide, but still blaring its horn. Once the driver regained control, he kept on going.

I realized I was lying in the lap of my rescuer, who had fallen with me onto the side of the road, a good place to have gotten squashed right along with me. My rescuer was brave as well as strong.

And she was a girl.

Which I realized when she yelled at the retreating car, "Hey!" Then, "Hey! Come back!" And—when that didn't get any reaction—"I have your license number, you creep!" Then, in a much gentler voice, she asked, "Are you all right? Are you hurt? Should somebody call a doctor?" all in a breathless rush.

I turned to look at a girl who couldn't have been any more than a couple years older than me—seventeen, eighteen at the most. She was dressed in a gauzy blue and white summer dress, her face pretty much as pale as the white of the stripes. "I'm all right," I managed to say, straightening my legs so I wasn't sitting on them. "You?"

She looked startled, then flashed a grin. "I think I feel the way you look," she told me.

Someone nearby started crying. Without glasses, my vision was okay enough to make out the form of another girl on the sidewalk behind us, probably a friend of my rescuer, because she said, "Oh, Eleni, I was sure I was about to see you get killed."

The girl who had saved me, Eleni, said, "We're both fine, Betsy." And, because her friend sounded like she was about to hyperventilate, "Come on, breathe deeply. Calm yourself."

The second girl, Betsy, fanned herself vigorously with a straw hat and took deep gulping breaths. I was clear witted enough to note that she was already wearing a hat, so I figured the one she was holding belonged to Eleni, who must have lost it in the scramble to save me.

Despite all her fanning, Betsy warned, "I think I'm feeling faint, Eleni."

"No, you're doing fine," Eleni reassured her. "Besides, if you faint, you'll drop the camera, and what will your father say then?"

Though this didn't make a whole lot of sense, it

seemed to be what Betsy needed to hear: some rea-son *not* to faint. She tightened her grip on the big, boxy camera she was holding, and her breathing be-came less quavery.

Just as I was thinking it really was time to stop this lying-down-in-the-street business, I was aware of someone crouching down beside us, and a male voice asked, "Did the car hit her?"

"I don't think so," Eleni said at the same time I sat up and said, "No."

It was the man with the bad suit, and he tried to hand me a stick.

Which made so little sense, I squinted to bring it into my seeing range. I recognized the object was not a stick but a piece of plastic, jagged at one end as though broken, with the other end curved. Something like, I thought, the earpiece of a pair of glasses.

"Damn!" I said.

Betsy gasped, "Golly!" Eleni looked shocked, like she'd never heard someone actually speak that word before.

The man looked disapproving but still spoke gently: "I'm afraid this is the biggest piece that's left of your glasses."

"I can't see anything without them!" I said. Which included, of course, the archway that had gotten me here. Not that I knew where *here* was, but obviously I'd done *something* wrong, so I needed to go back around and try again.

Thank you, Larry. Thank you very much. "It transports you where you want to go." Yeah, right, you little blue freak.

What I WANTED was to go home.

Though Eleni tried to make me stay put, saying, "Maybe you should just—" I got to my feet. My jeans had ripped at both knees, and my right knee was bleeding, though not emergency-room-quantity bleeding. And the palms of my hands stung. They were scraped and had gravel embedded in them. None of that stopped me from jumping back up onto the sidewalk and looking for the gate.

Nothing.

From either direction.

Of course not. I needed my special glasses to see such things.

I tried stepping through where the arch had been, at the edge of the curb. *Home, home, home,* I thought, picturing my own room.

Nothing.

I tried stepping through with my eyes closed, thinking maybe not seeing the wrong reality might somehow affect something—or some such: How was *I* supposed to know how magic worked? Hey, I was desperate.

Bad-Suit Man caught me when I nearly toppled off the curb again.

"Is she all right?" asked one of the bystanders, maybe the woman with the child, too far away for me to make out now, with my limited eyesight.

"I'm fine," I insisted, sounding more snappish than I intended. I headed farther into the street without even looking, so it was a good thing it wasn't a busy street and the few cars on it had all stopped at my recent near-accident. I figured the occupants were still watching, maybe expecting a delayed-reaction fatality.

I found one lens, which was all cracked, but I thought maybe it would still let me see well enough to find the elusive archway. But when I went to pick it up, the pieces fell loose, pieces about as big as shredded carrots in a salad. I searched for the other lens but couldn't find it.

The girl who had rescued me came up behind, putting one hand on my shoulder and taking hold of my opposite elbow with the other. "Why don't you sit down on this nice lady's porch?" she suggested, pulling me out of the street into someone's yard.

An old woman with gray hair that had a definite tinge of blue to it and who was wearing a housedress (no hat, the anal-retentive part of me noted) held open the screen door to her house. But my knees were going all shaky on me, and I wouldn't make it that far. I sat down heavily on the concrete step outside.

"I've called for an ambulance," the old lady said. "Did the car hit her? Is that a piece of metal sticking out of her?"

I remembered the accident victim I'd seen, long, long ago this morning, patting his chest, asking, "Is the steering wheel column sticking out again?" and I wondered if I was in shock and only *thought* the car had missed me. The old woman was close enough that, by squinting, I could see where her eyes were looking.

"Holy moley," Eleni muttered.

Anticipating seeing the car's fender sticking out of my abdomen, I checked—but it was only my belly-button ring. I tugged my shirt down over the top of my jeans.

"I don't need an ambulance," I told everyone. I rested my face in my hands. How could I ever get home if I couldn't see the way? What was the matter with that mini-munchkin-gone-bad Larry, not giving me better instructions? "Larry?" I called. Had he come through with me? "Larry, if you're here, you come out this instant."

"Who's Larry?" Eleni asked.

If my jeans and my belly-button ring were getting weird looks, talking about little blue guys was sure to get me committed. "Nobody," I assured her.

"Let me get you a washcloth for your poor head," the old woman said.

"I don't need one," I told her.

Betsy, who had joined us from across the street, murmured, "I could use a cold cloth, please," and she followed the old woman back into the house.

Because I hate to wear glasses, over the years I've gotten good at extrapolating things about my surroundings without the benefit of actually seeing much. I was aware of a small crowd at the edge of the old lady's yard, with one person significantly shorter than the others—probably the little girl I'd glimpsed before. It had just struck me that the murmur of their voices sounded more disapproving than sympathetic, when the child's shrill voice raised above the others, demanding, "Mommy, why is she dressed so funny?"

There were some titters from the crowd.

The answer, while still rather quiet, was louder than the previous murmuring had been. Louder and disapproving: "I don't know, honey. Maybe she's a farmworker."

Like anyone would wear Abercrombie jeans to work on a farm.

Encouraged by the obvious amusement of her elders, the little girl said, "Her pants are so tight, if she bent over to feed the chickens, she'd bust right out of them."

More tittering.

Any mother-daughter team wearing white gloves and hats outside of an Easter parade should *not* consider themselves the fashion police, but—being stranded here—I didn't have the heart or energy to tell them what I thought of them.

Eleni, however, went to the fence. I heard her coo, "My, what a lovely little girl you have there, ma'am." Then, just as sweetly, she asked, "Do you ever plan to teach her human kindness, or were you intending on raising a poisonous little hyena?"

This did not endear her to them nearly as much as it did to me.

The mother spoke to her child, saying, "These are both obviously *bad* girls, dear," and she tugged on her child's arm and dragged her away.

Eleni put her hands on her hips, and the rest of the crowd dispersed, obviously unwilling to risk her turning her wrath onto any of them.

Even Mr. Tweed-Suit Man, who had crossed back over to this side of the street again, was heading for the corner when Eleni called him back, demanding, "What if we need you?"

He returned, opened his satchel, and handed me a card.

I squinted and read:

BUZZ A. TINNELL
FULLER BRUSH SALESMAN
TELEPHONE NUMBER: IDLEWILD 6-0296

Things were weird, but I was perplexed at just how weird. I looked from Eleni to the man and asked, "You want me to buy a brush?"

Eleni took the card and tucked it into a pocket of her gauzy summer dress. "This is if you need another witness, an adult."

Well, that clarification didn't help a whole lot.

She gestured down the street. "To testify that that driver never even stopped to see if you were hurt."

Okay, then. But that was *not* number one on my list of worries.

I was aware of Eleni sitting down on the stoop next to me. "I'll stay with you," she assured me, which I realized meant the salesman had left as soon as I wasn't looking, eager to be about his Fuller-Brushing where there were no delusional accident victims or sharp-tongued rescuers.

I had my head in my hands again, so all I could see was the bottom part of my rescuer's leg, with her dress billowing around her feet. She was wearing high heels. I was thinking about telling her that she shouldn't be sitting on the concrete step in her good clothes when finally I recognized the blue and white striped dress—one of a kind, handmade in Italy.

Finally I took a good look at her face.

And *finally* I recognized that, too.

Despite the wrong name, Eleni was my grandmother.

14

In the Wrong Place
at the Wrong Time

L arry had said the arch would transport me to where I wanted to go, and I had gone and let my mind wander for an instant—as though picturing Gia and Nana sitting together looking at the photo album wasn't reckless enough—to picturing the photos themselves. Which is not to say it wasn't Larry's fault that I ended up smack in the 1950s.

"Larry, you ought to be flushed down a toilet," I muttered.

Eleni—Nana—raised her eyebrows at me. Her dark-colored, young eyebrows. Nana's name was *Helen*, not *Eleni*, but how could I not have recognized her? I'd seen pictures of her as a child and as a young woman, but I always thought of Nana as she'd always looked to me. Now here she was with her skin un-wrinkled; her shoulder-length hair bouncy and dark rather than in the short, permed, and gray style which was all I'd ever known; and she was slim, though for as long back as I could remember, she'd always been a bit…roundish. The aides at the nursing home were always saying how attractive she'd been as a young woman, but—as much as I loved her—to me she was attractive in a grandmotherly way, not as the kind of girl who would turn heads at her high school. Yet here she was every bit as gorgeous as Tiffanie Mills—and I mean on one of Tiffanie's good days.

Now, my young grandmother was looking at me with worry in her eyes, and she assured me, "Help will be here soon."

"I don't need help," I told her. Well, I did, but not the kind she meant. I could hear the faintest wail of a siren approaching. That was the last thing I needed: to be taken off to a hospital, to have people start asking questions. I scrambled to my feet. "I've got to get out of here," I said.

"No, it's okay," Eleni said. She tugged on my arm to try to get me to sit down again. "The ambulance will be here in another two minutes."

Which was exactly the point.

Eleni seemed to realize that. She tipped her head and looked at me quizzically. "What's wrong?" she asked.

"I've got to get out of here," I repeated.

Again the eyebrows went up. But what she asked was, "Are you sure? You may well have hit your head when you fell, and someone should take a look at that knee in case you need stitches."

She must have seen my answer in my expression.

"Well," she said, "obviously I can't just let you run off all alone after that brush with death," which sounded like the prelude to an argument with me. But instead, she swept to her feet. "Come on this way, then." She took my arm and hustled me down the front path to the sidewalk.

"Doing all right?" she asked, and—when I nodded—she led me down the street, around the corner, down another street, around another corner. Her heels made a rapid *click, click, click* on the sidewalk, a sound that brought back memories of when I'd been much younger and she'd been well and active, a sound I associated with her, because I pretty much live in sneakers and my mother wears flats—my father as well as her current husband being on the short side. Despite her heels, it was me, with my sore knee, who had trouble keeping up.

"There's a little park on the next block," Eleni said.

It was the first time I realized where we were, since the park—one of those urban, one-block affairs with a few trees, two benches, one drinking fountain, and a statue of some Civil War guy—is still there today, three blocks from where Nana used to live. Which, by the way—thank you very much, Larry—is nowhere near Westfall Nursing Home.

"Sure, I remember this place," I said, squinting as I looked around, and had the sense not to add, *You used to bring me here when I was a little kid.*

Eleni sat me down on one of the benches, then tugged at the hole in my jeans to get a peek at my knee. "I think," she told me, "once you stop moving, it'll stop bleeding." She gave me an of-course-that-is-not-to-say-I-approve look. From her pocket, she got a handkerchief—not a tissue, but an embroidered cloth handkerchief—which she proclaimed as being "mostly clean," and went to moisten it at the fountain.

As soon as she was out of hearing, I whispered fiercely, "Larry!" No answer. Of course, without my glasses I wouldn't be able to see him or—as part of the weirdness of those glasses—to hear him, but that didn't mean he couldn't make his toxic little presence known. "Larry, you better get that little blue butt of yours out here immediately," I said.

Eleni cleared her throat, making me jump, since I hadn't been aware of her returning, and she sat down beside me. But maybe she hadn't heard me after all, because she didn't comment and only concentrated on my knee. "This *will* need better looking after," she told me sternly as she picked gravel out of the wound.

It stung like crazy, but I figured that was the least of my worries.

"Are you sure you didn't strike your head?" she asked me.

"Positive," I assured her. "If I'm acting a bit like a spaz, it's only because I can't see much without my glasses."

She glanced up at me, but I couldn't tell what I'd said wrong. "Uh-huh," she said, not sounding at all convinced. Then she said, "Well, so let me introduce myself: My name is Eleni."

"Eleni," I repeated. I was supposed to call my nana "Eleni"?

She grinned. "Well, actually it's Helen, but 'Eleni' is the Greek way of saying it."

"But we're not Greek," I blurted before catching myself.

Luckily, she must have assumed I meant "we" as a nation rather than "we" as a family, or maybe she just figured I meant to say "you." She shrugged and said, "Helen is...well, honestly, it's a grandmother's name."

I tried not to choke. The one thing it showed was that I was not the only one in my family who would have preferred a sexy name. I wondered if there was a Greek equivalent to "Wendy" and guessed probably not.

"So," she prompted. "And you are...?"

We were on dangerous ground. What if I did or said something that changed history? *Hello. I'm Wendy, and I'm your granddaughter, and I accidentally came back to the 1950s, and now I'm looking for a way back.* It might be enough to scare her out of ever having children, and then I'd never be born.

I'd already hesitated too long to just make something up, and she was looking at my T-shirt, emblazoned with the Nike name and trademark swoosh. "Nick," she misread, then corrected it to "Nike," saying it with only one syllable, to rhyme with "like." "Surely that's not your name?"

"No," I admitted.

She waited another moment. "Hit your head and can't remember, or don't want to say?"

"I'd like to tell you"—I couldn't bring myself to call Nana "Eleni"—"but I can't."

"Okay," she said agreeably. "A secret is better than not being able to remember. If you couldn't remember, I'd have to get help whether you wanted me to or not. But I can't just call you 'Hey you' or 'Nike.'"

While I tried to think of something, she suggested, "How about 'Jeannette'?"

My mother's name. I remembered how that had been the first serious sign of her Alzheimer's—when she couldn't keep me and my mother straight. I tried to keep my voice neutral as I asked, "Why 'Jeannette'?"

Eleni shrugged. "I've always liked the name. Kind of French, but not too much. I have a stuffed bear named Jeannette. Actually, if I ever get married, I plan to name my first child Jeannette, so I'm really hoping it'll be a daughter and not a son."

I had to laugh.

"There, then. It's settled. So, I'm assuming, Jeannette, that you don't want me to contact the police and tell them about the man who almost ran you down?"

"I'm the dork who fell off the curb," I said.

I guessed by the long look she gave me that there weren't dorks in the 1950s. Or, more likely, there were, but they were called something else. "Well," she countered, "but he should have stopped."

"Besides," I said, "all I could say was that it was a big gray car. That's not much to go on, but I don't know cars. I can't even keep straight which is a van and which is an SUV."

From her somewhat dazed expression, I gathered at least one or the other of those had not yet been invented.

"Oldsmobile," Eleni finally said. "The hood ornament is quite distinctive. License number M13487."

To fill in the silence, I said, "I can't see much without my glasses."

She nodded as if saying, *Okay, well, I'll buy that for now.*

"How can you remember the number?"

"*M* for Monroe County, then *1* because he was so self-centered and was only thinking of himself; *3*—that's you, me, and Betsy; add all those numbers together to get *4;* add all the numbers so far together to get *8;* but the driver took off, so you subtract the first number from the last number to get *7:* M13487."

This game with numbers from the grandmother who could no longer remember her own name.

"You know," I said, "I don't even know what you just said."

She shrugged.

"Anyway," I repeated, "it was my own fault."

"And you don't want to involve the police," she guessed.

I didn't say anything because there was nothing to say.

"Are you in trouble," she asked, "or is it your friend, Larry?"

Being of quick mind and sharp wit, I said, "Huh?"

"Because I will tell you something," Eleni said, "Betsy was taking a picture of me"—she gave a dismissive wave of her hand, and blushed as she explained all in a rush—"because she wants to send a picture of me to her cousin so that he'll come here for August and stay with her parents rather than going to his other aunt and uncle in Sodus before he enlists in the army..." She hesitated, obviously embarrassed at the thought of using her picture to tempt a young man into summering in Rochester—and meanwhile I tried not to wonder if the young man in question was Papa: What I did *not* need to do was to influence *anything* that had already happened. "Anyway," she continued, "so Betsy was facing me, and I was facing the spot where you..." She hesitated again, this time groping for the right words. "The spot where one second you weren't. And then you were."

I used that time-honored tradition of taking a moment to scratch my head while I tried to come up with some believable explanation. "You must have blinked," I said.

Eleni laughed. "No," she said firmly. "Try again."

"Maybe the flash blinded you?"

Ignoring my babbling, she told me suddenly, "You look very much like my sister, who died."

"I am not a ghost," I informed her.

For a moment she looked annoyed. "I didn't say I thought you were her. Besides, *if* Mathilda came back to Earth, which I don't for a moment think she might, I can't believe the first thing she would do would be to step into the path of an oncoming car. I just meant: There's a strong resemblance." She tipped her head and looked closely at me. "You look like me, too."

Don't I wish, I thought.

She finished, "Almost as though, maybe, we're related..."

I was willing to go so far as to admit, "I suppose I could be from some very distant branch of your family."

"Except none of us can pop into existence like something out of a Flash Gordon movie."

"I don't know Flash Gordon," I said.

"Don't try to change the subject."

Once again she tipped her head and scrutinized me. "You dress oddly...," she said, which I guess I did in a world of pastel shirtwaist dresses and white gloves and hats, "and you speak rather oddly, too..."—and here I'd been congratulating myself on avoiding such dated references as manned space flights, Snoop Dogg, or SPAM as anything besides lunch meat. My grandmother asked, "So are you a crazy person who by coincidence just happens to look like a family member...?" Her eyes grew wide as a new thought came to her. "You're not from this time!" she gasped. "You're a time traveler from the future." She gave another gasp. "Are you the daughter I'm going to have?"

"No," I said, wondering how—in minutes—she had come to the conclusion that I had most needed to keep her from.

"Granddaughter?" she pressed.

"No," I said, but perhaps not so passionately as before, for she leaned back with a self-satisfied look on her face.

"So what have you come back from the future to warn me about?"

"Nothing," I protested.

She was sitting there, considering—I could tell—

analyzing her life, trying to second-guess herself, attempting to figure out what she had done that she shouldn't have, or what she hadn't done that she should have, which had caused disastrous enough results that a messenger had been sent through time to intervene. I'd seen enough *Star Trek* reruns to know how the slightest change I caused here could escalate to dangerous proportions by my time—if my time ever arrived now that I'd blundered into my own family history.

"Eleni, please," I begged. "Pretend I'm not here. You haven't done anything wrong or caused anything bad to happen."

"Then why did you come here?" she asked.

It seemed safest to tell her the truth. "By accident," I said.

She gave me that skeptical look I was coming to recognize. So, without exactly admitting I was her granddaughter, I told her everything about the glasses, how I'd found them, the strange things they let me see. The one part I didn't tell her was about Westfall Nursing Home. What could I say? *One day, you will be old, and your mind will fail?* But I explained how Julian had followed me, and how, by running away from him, I'd found myself in a new world. I told about the elves who had captured him, and about that little blue blot on the universe, Larry, and how he'd led me to believe that all I needed to get home was to click my heels three times and say, "There's no place like home."

"Gee whiz," Eleni said slowly when I'd finally finished, which sounded like one of those cute, mild fifties expressions. I didn't have the heart to tell her what *whiz* means today. She said, "Okay, explain again about this elf fellow Julian."

"What?" I said. "Specifically?"

"Why are you assuming the worst about him?"

"Excuse me?" I said.

"It just seems like you abandoned him in a very bad situation."

"Maybe," I admitted.

She gave me a look that I recognized from when I'd been five years old and claimed an intruder must have broken into the house and stolen the cookies Nana had told me were for *after* dinner.

"All right," I conceded. "Probably. But I'm not sure what that has to do with anything."

"I'm just trying to understand. So he began going to your school in September, was always kind of quiet, never caused any trouble. Showed concern when he thought you were shaken up from the bus accident."

"He was after my glasses," I interrupted.

"Could you have stopped him from grabbing them away from you when you were outside the nurse's office?" Eleni asked. "All alone? Just the two of you?"

"Hmmm," I said.

"Sounds to me like he didn't know about them till after this Tiffanie girl told him. How long have you known her? Did she go to grammar school with you?"

Grammar school? I didn't know if that meant elementary, middle, junior high, or high, but rather than admit that, I just explained, "I met her in ninth grade."

"And so she's made your life miserable since then?"

What *was* she getting at? Slowly, hesitantly, I said, "No."

"Generally a mean-spirited girl, is she?"

"Not really," I had to say. "She's, you know, a cheerleader type." Did they have cheerleaders in the 1950s? "You know, pretty, popular, never really pays attention to anybody not in her crowd. Not the worst of the type," I had to admit.

Eleni said, "So it wasn't until you saw her looking ugly that you came to distrust her?"

That was making me sound like the kind of girl who makes friends only with attractive people, and pokes fun at the rest. Was that what I was like? Not only a coward, but a small-minded coward? "She was *old* and ugly," I told Eleni. "She looked like a witch."

Eleni raised her eyebrows at me. "So you distrust Julian for being too good-looking, and Tiffanie for not being good-looking enough."

"They're not human," I said, "and they're trying to pass themselves off as though they are."

"Which is a bad thing," Eleni said in a tone somewhere in between statement and question.

"Depending on their purpose." Was she trying to tell me I was some sort of image bigot?

"At this point we don't know their purpose," Eleni said. "All we know is that Julian could have revealed your hiding place and exposed you to the kind of people who get themselves into a mob of five, beat up an unarmed man, and try to kill an intelligent creature no more than a fraction of their size."

"Well, intelligent may be overstating it for Larry," I protested.

Eleni stood up. "Excuse me," she said.

For a moment I thought she was so thoroughly disgruntled with my bad attitude that she was abandoning me. By squinting and extrapolating, I could tell she'd gone up to the drinking fountain on the other side of the Civil War general and fiddled with the mechanism; then she came back. "The water was stuck on," she explained. "I hate to waste. Where were we?"

"You were telling me I'm a weenie."

Eleni looked startled and said, "I'm sure I wasn't."

I reworded it: "You were telling me that I jumped to conclusions about Tiffanie and Julian based on appearances, and that I assumed Julian was bad since he's obviously different, and so I did nothing to help him when he was confronted with people who were almost for-sure bad."

That, Eleni was willing to nod at. But then, looking distracted, she again said, "Excuse me." She returned to the fountain and smacked it. When she came back to the bench, she told me, "I'm guessing the key to getting you back to your own time is to rescue Julian."

"I don't see that. And *seeing* is the point entirely, I guess. Because, without those glasses, getting back to Julian is as impossible as getting back home."

It was Eleni's turn to go "Hmmm." Then she said, "So where could those glasses have come from, anyway, to end up on your front lawn? If we could figure that out, maybe we could get you another pair."

"Maybe, maybe not," I said, which was actually a lot more optimistic than I felt.

Eleni stared off into space, trying to think of a solution, then suddenly snapped, "What *is* the matter with that fountain? It seems to have developed a mind of its own—a pigheaded, disagreeable mind."

And with a lead-in line like that, how could I not finally catch on?

This time, *I* went. When I got near the fountain, I could see it was spurting high into the air—like if a normal-sized person was holding a finger over the spigot.

Or if a chipmunk-sized person was holding his little blue butt in the way of the water flow. "Larry!" I cried.

I looked into the fountain. And found my one remaining lens sitting in the water waiting for me.

15

The Relative Sizes of Hearts

The spray of water was squirting high into the air off to my left, so I was able to pick my lens out of the bowl of the fountain. I was using the hem of my T-shirt as a drying cloth when the water veered right, nailing me between the eyes.

A moment later the water turned off.

"Yeah, you demented little blueberry," I muttered as I resumed wiping, "and if you're thinking of claiming that was an accident, don't even bother."

I held the lens up to my right eye. I've never mastered winking; I can just barely manage to keep my right eye open with my left eye closed, though not vice versa.

The world came back into focus, including a soggy Larry, sitting on the edge of the drinking fountain. "Of course it was an accident," he told me, sounding as sincere as someone trying to sell something in an infomercial. "Water is slippery; it made me slip." He added, "You look like a pirate, squinting that way: Ahoy, maties! Anyone seen my parrot? Arr, arr." He made a very disagreeable face which was probably supposed to reflect how I looked, with his eyes squeezed tightly shut and his mouth drooping open foolishly.

Before I had a chance to demonstrate to him some of water's other qualities—like the ability to drown little blue smart-mouths—Eleni came up behind me. "Is he really here?" she asked in an awed voice. "Larry?"

"You bet your sweet bottom I'm here," Larry told her, giving a big, noisy air kiss.

"*Don't* talk to her like that," I warned him, grateful that without the glasses she could neither see nor hear him.

He clicked his heels and saluted sharply. *"Jawohl, mein Kapitän!"* he assured me. But then he held his hand up by the side of his mouth—a shield, as though that would prevent me from seeing—and made kissy lips at my grandmother.

"What's he saying?" Eleni asked.

"I'm in love," Larry moaned.

"Nothing," I told her. To Larry, I said, "If you can't behave yourself, I won't help you."

"You!" he hooted. "Help *me*?" He laughed so hard, he rolled off the edge of the water fountain and had to use his wings to keep aloft. As they were a bit waterlogged, he had to flap like crazy just to slow his descent. He looked less like a graceful hummingbird than like a dodo who hasn't been told that dodos can't fly.

"Correct me if I'm wrong," I said in my most superior tone, "but you only tried to get our attention once"—I caught myself in time not to say "Nana"—"once Eleni expressed concern for Julian. You wanted me to *stay* to help him, so now I'm thinking you want me to *go back* to help him. And that's the only reason you rescued my lens: on the off chance that I might do what you wanted."

Larry had wafted down to the ground and he was shaking his wings like a dog drying itself off. "Maybe" was all he would admit to.

"May I look?" Eleni asked.

"The lens is matched to my prescription," I said.

Larry gave a snort and said, "The lens lets anybody see."

I hesitated before passing that information along to Eleni. "He's rude and crude," I added, reluctantly handing the lens to her.

Eleni gave me a like-you're-not? look which reminded me that teenagers in the 1950s spoke differently from teenagers in my time. She put the lens up to her right eye. "Neat-o!" she said. Then she leaned slightly forward and asked, "May I?"

Larry must have said yes because she extended her left hand out, palm up.

Yuck! I thought, realizing she must have let him climb onto her hand. *I* wouldn't trust him that close to me, but then, I'd known him longer.

She straightened, with her hand in front of her face, obviously listening to him.

And listening to him.

And listening to him...

"What's he saying?" I demanded.

I expected her to answer, "Nothing" to demonstrate how annoying I'd been, but she told me, "He said Julian and his side of the family are much more benevolent rulers than Berrech and his crowd would be. And that the current rulers have a hands-off-the-humans policy which we"—she indicated her and me—"should be aware of before you"—now pointing at me—"ask, 'So what?' He's also saying it would be a lot easier to explain things if both of us could see and hear him at the same time."

That needed a moment to sink in. As we only had one lens, I guessed, "Oh, so he wants *you* to come through the arch, too."

She raised her eyebrow at me, and I realized that my tone could, maybe, have been taken as insulting.

"I mean," I explained myself, "it's probably a dangerous thing to ever suspect Larry of acting altruistically."

Eleni handed the lens back to me, keeping her other palm outstretched for Larry. "He says his heart is broken."

When I looked through the lens, Larry was sitting cross-legged on Eleni's palm. He told me, "I like her a lot better than I like you."

"That's fine," I said. "I don't like you at all."

"Stop bickering," Eleni said. "The two of you sound like my cousins, who aren't old enough to go to school yet."

Probably sounding even more like those cousins, I complained, "Do not," and was irritated that Larry muttered the exact same thing at the exact same time.

"What you need to do," Eleni said, "is ask him: If we go to this Elfland, or whatever it's called, can we each return to our own separate homes?"

I tried to hand the lens back to her, but she shook her head. "You know him better. You have to be the judge whether he's telling the truth."

Larry clapped his hands to his heart and cried, "Wounded! Her harsh words have wounded me!"

"Well, that's one in the I-don't-believe-him column," I warned.

"Kazaran Dahaani," he said.

"What?"

"Where we were. It's not 'Elfland,' which, excuse me, girls, is a pretty lame excuse for a name. The place is called Kazaran Dahaani. Put that in the why-would-he-lie-about-THAT? column."

Having learned firsthand how frustrating it was to be left out of the conversation, I told Eleni, "He says the place I met him is called...ahm...Caravan Salami—"

"Kazaran Dahaani," Larry corrected wearily, like he wasn't speaking a foreign language I had never heard before and I should have gotten it the first time.

"Kazaran Dahaani," I repeated. To Larry, I said, "All right: If Eleni and I go back to Kazaran Dahaani—" All fluttery, he got to his feet. "Now don't get your little blue self excited," I cautioned. "All I said was 'if.' *If* we go there just long enough to hear you out. *If* we go, whether or not we decide to stay to help Julian. If we do that, will we be able to go back home: Eleni here, and me to my place and time?"

"Yes," Larry assured me with an emphatic nod.

While I weighed the sincerity of his answer, Eleni said, "Find out what went wrong last time."

"Yeah," I said. "How did I end up here?"

"You must have been thinking about your grand-mother at this age," Larry answered.

Chagrined that he'd figured out our relationship, and not daring to ask him to please not tell her—since I suspected that would be the single most likely thing he'd do if he knew I dreaded it—I asked, "Uh-huh, so if I'd been thinking of Big Bird, I would have ended up on *Sesame Street*?"

"No," Larry sneered. "I hate to be the one to break this to you, but *Sesame Street* is a made-up place. The closest you could have gotten was the soundstage where it's filmed."

"Big Bird?" Eleni asked, but I ignored her and countered Larry's statement by demanding, "And Kazaran Dahaani is real?"

"Duh." Larry glanced longingly at Eleni. "I really prefer—"

"I don't care if you prefer talking to her," I told him. "I'm the one with the lens."

He crossed his arms and sat back down again on Eleni's outstretched palm with a sulky "Lucky me."

"Don't you mutter at me," I warned him, realizing even as I said it that I was sounding like my own mother. "I never heard of Kazaran Dahaani," I continued. "I was definitely *not* wishing about, thinking about, or picturing in my mind any place like that."

"Duh," Larry said. Boy, that's annoying, you know? He explained, "Kazaran Dahaani is the default setting."

"Default setting," I repeated for Eleni's benefit, then snapped at Larry, "Okay—what's *that* mean?"

With the singsong enthusiasm of one of those *Sesame Street* characters we'd just been talking about announcing the letter of the day, Larry explained, "Every other time you pass through a gate, you come out at Kazaran Dahaani. Or, to put it another way: Starting from Kazaran Dahaani, you can get anywhere. But, starting from anywhere, you get to Kazaran Dahaani. So..." he continued, now in a condescending, lecturing tone, "before you ask...no, you would not be able to go directly to your home from here: You have to pass through Kazaran Dahaani first."

"I don't know...," I said.

Eleni, reacting to my skepticism, asked, "You think he's lying?"

Larry crossed his heart and put a finger to his lips,

all the while wearing a solemn expression that practically screamed, *Of course, I'm lying!*

"I don't know," I repeated.

"Your other choice," Larry pointed out, "is to stay here."

"Yeah," I said, "I—" I sighed. "I pretty much have to trust you because I can't stay here. But there's no reason for Eleni to put herself in danger by following you anywhere."

"Except," Larry said, "that she's smarter than you, she's braver than you, and she has a bigger heart than you. You're much more likely to succeed if she's helping you. Besides, if she stayed here, you'd probably squirm out of helping Julian. You'd go back home instead, now that I've rescued you."

Never.

Well . . . possibly.

Okay, okay, probably.

I didn't point out that I wouldn't have needed rescuing if he hadn't walked off with the lens.

"What's he saying?" Eleni asked.

"You're braver than me and smarter than me, and he trusts you more than he trusts me."

"So you think it's safe to go?" she asked.

"No," I told her. "Besides, there's no reason for you to get involved."

"To help you," she said.

"Once I'm there, I'll be able to see perfectly well even without the glasses," I reminded her. "Kazaran Dahaani might suck in the hospitality category, but it gives me twenty-twenty eyesight."

She gave that slow allowances-must-be-made-for-this-person nod I was beginning to recognize. *What?* I wanted to ask. *What?*

"Yes," she said. "But you'll still probably need help."

I couldn't tell if she said that because she figured I was inept and couldn't rescue Julian, or because she figured I was a weasel and wouldn't even try.

If I admitted that I was only planning on passing through Kazaran Dahaani on my way home, I suspected she would try to rescue Julian on her own. Larry was right: She had a bigger heart than me, and she was braver.

As for smarter: I'd have to wait to see if we survived this adventure she was pushing me into before I decided on that.

16

So Close...

S o," Eleni asked, "should we go back to where I first saw you?" Looking worried, she added, "Because Betsy's probably wondering what happened to us. She has a bit of an overactive imagination so she's probably trying to convince the ambulance crew that the only explanation for us being gone is that you must have staged everything just to provide an opportunity to separate us so you could kidnap me."

Oh, boy. Like my grandmother couldn't have a *rational* friend?

But before I could put my foot into my mouth with that, Larry said, "No use going back there, anyway."

I held up a finger for Eleni to wait and asked Larry, "Why not?"

"No gate there."

"You know," I told him, "you can be incredibly annoying. What do you mean 'no gate'? I just—*we* just—came through there."

Larry sighed like someone who was being asked for the seventeenth time to explain something. Something obvious. "You went through the gate in Kazaran Dahaani."

"Yes...," I said to him.

In a very condescending tone, he quoted himself from earlier: "From Kazaran Dahaani to anywhere."

"Yes..." My aggravation level was escalating beyond my ability to hide it.

He stood on Eleni's palm, which she was trying to hold steady, and not doing a wonderful job of it as she couldn't see him. If it had been me, Larry would have been making snide remarks. He put his little blue hand on his hip, like a cross between a sea captain on a storm-tossed deck and a disgruntled interior decorator, and said, "Well, so, like, you think there are gates everywhere?"

"Isn't that what 'From Kazaran Dahaani to anywhere' means?"

He rolled his tiny little eyes, probably unaware

NOW YOU SEE IT . . .

how much this made him look like an impatient
hamster. Like an annoying impatient hamster. Like a
blue annoying impatient hamster. Okay, so I guess he
didn't look much like a hamster at all. But he did
have beady little eyes that he rolled at me. He explained, "There are a limited number of permanent
gates built on your world. You probably came
through one to get *to* Kazaran Dahaani."

"Probably," I repeated.

"What's he saying?" Eleni asked.

"Gibberish," I told her.

"Technical stuff," Larry corrected me, which I
figured was just his excuse for being incoherent.
"When you wished to be here," he said, "an opening
formed exactly where you wished to be." Although
I'd finally caught on, he slowed down even more and
enunciated oh-so-carefully: "A temporary opening."

I told Eleni, "Temporary hole in the space-time
continuum, or some such." Addressing Larry, I
asked, "So how do we get back?"

"Duh," he said. "Didn't I just explain that the
first gate you came through was probably one of the
permanent ones?"

"Define 'probably,'" I said.

"The temporary gates only last a few moments.
So either someone from Kazaran Dahaani had just

come out when you happened to stumble upon it, or it was a permanent gate."

I told Eleni, "He says the way I came through has closed, so to get back we need to go through the gate that's in the garden at Westfall Nursing Home."

She asked, "Where's Westfall Nursing Home?" and I was relieved she didn't ask what I'd been doing at a nursing home.

I said, "South and Robinson."

She looked as though she was trying to picture it in her head, and I figured South is a major road but Robinson is a side street, so I clarified, "Near the expressway."

"Expressway," she repeated in a perplexed tone that made me guess 490 must have been built after the 1950s.

"Ahmm, across from Highland Park?" I suggested.

"We'll have to take a bus."

"Okay." I dug into my pocket to see if I had any money for bus fare, and remembered that I had spent the last of my allowance in the cafeteria. My mother—a liberated twenty-first-century mom—believes high schoolers should be capable of making or providing for their own lunch, and I hadn't had time to make a sandwich.

Apparently that oops-I'm-broke expression hadn't

changed in the intervening years. "Bus fare is a dime," Eleni said. "I can cover both of us."

I didn't tell her that, in my time, just about all a dime was good for was to use as an emergency screwdriver when the backs of the chairs in the cafeteria got wobbly enough to annoy. I only said, "Larry, you're on your own, because if Eleni walks around with her hand out like that, people are going to think she's begging for change."

Larry flew off her hand and landed on her shoulder. "Now *you* look like a pirate," I told Eleni, "with a psychotic bluebird instead of a parrot."

She gave me that increasingly familiar oh-dear-what's-the-matter-with-her-now? look and I remembered she hadn't been able to hear him when he'd been doing his pirate routine.

"Arr, arr," Larry said.

I sighed. "Never mind."

Luckily, the bus stop was only a block away; and, even luckier, we only had a short wait before a bus rolled up in a cloud of diesel fumes and hiss of air brakes.

"Behave yourself," I warned Larry before putting the lens into my pocket lest the people on the bus think I was playing at being the stereotypical monocled Nazi villain.

Well, without my glasses it was hard to tell what they thought, but the driver certainly seemed to be wearing a disapproving stare. He probably worried I was one of those people who would start talking loudly to myself and make the other passengers nervous. Eleni and I sat halfway back, behind a woman wearing a hat with big feather flowers on it. She clicked her tongue in a definitely disapproving way and sniffed as though testing the air to affirm her suspicion that someone who looked as bad as me must stink.

"Let me know when we get there," Eleni said, and we didn't dare say anything else for fear of being overheard.

I looked out the window, which was mostly a blur without glasses; but I could see well enough to note that there was a lot less to Rochester in the 1950s than what I was used to—less traffic, fewer buildings, and the buildings that were there were not so close together. *What if,* I suddenly wondered, *Westfall Nursing Home hasn't been built yet?* Eleni hadn't recognized the name. I told myself that there was no reason she should be familiar with the area nursing homes, but found it hard to ignore the dread that started squeezing me, whispering at me that there was no telling what I'd find. *And how old was the gate*

I passed through? I asked myself. What if the elves had only built it recently? I wished that I could ask Larry whether he'd be able to find another gate if the one we were looking for wasn't there or wasn't accessible.

Out of the corner of my eye, I saw something flutter, and I wondered if I'd been hanging around Larry so long he was becoming visible to me even without the lens. But when I looked straight on, there was no sign of him. I glanced at Eleni, but she was looking up and off to the side across the aisle, reading the advertisements over the bus's windows.

Something else fluttered and landed on my knee, not a vision or a wraith, after all. It was a feather, a feather flower petal. The hat of the woman seated ahead of us was molting.

Another feather petal drifted kneeward.

The next time, I was looking directly at the hat when I saw one of the petals stand upright, then jerk upward before it descended.

Less like molting, and more like being plucked.

Carefully, surreptitiously, I got the lens out of my pocket and brought it up to my eye just in time to see Larry, standing on the brim of the hat, yank another petal free.

"Stop it," I hissed.

Eleni glanced at me.

So did the woman with the hat.

I quickly removed the lens from in front of my eye and tried to give a reassuring that's-okay-I'm-really-mostly-harmless smile.

Before turning forward once more, the woman sniffed again as though sure that, eventually, she would discern a disagreeable odor coming from me.

Another petal bit the dust.

Eleni, of course, was watching me and so she missed it. In an intense undertone that was not meant to carry, I whispered, "Knock it off, Larry."

Eleni put her hand over mine and shook her head, warning me not to attract attention. The woman ahead of us glanced around again, probably assuming Eleni was trying to keep the poor schizo-phrenic calm.

"It's okay," I muttered.

Once again the woman faced forward, her back stiff with tension.

I handed the lens to Eleni, but obviously Larry had moved. She held it to her eye, looked discreetly around the bus, shrugged, then handed the lens back to me. I put it up to my eye just as Larry came back from wherever he'd been and landed on the lady's hat. I made a grab for him, but he shot out of there and I caught hold of one of the feathery blossoms instead.

The woman, who'd apparently been unable to feel Larry's weight, felt mine. She squealed and whipped around in her seat. Because I was holding the flower, the hat stayed stationary while her head rotated beneath it.

The *hair* stayed where it was, too, so that the side edge of her pageboy hairdo now covered one eye and came to her nose.

"Sorry," I said, hoping she hadn't noticed her wiggy secret had been revealed. Even as I spoke, I immediately let go of the flower.

Except that, weakened and made loose because of the petals Larry had already removed, the flower pretty much deconstructed in my hand. Petals wafted down toward the floor as all three of us—the woman, Eleni, and I—watched.

"You wretched person," the woman scolded me.

What could I say? *It wasn't me. It was a little blue spreenie.*

"Yes," I said. "I'm sorry."

Eleni leaned forward and straightened the woman's hat. "As good as new," she whispered, then assured her, "Nobody noticed."

No, it was pure coincidence that all the other passengers were facing in our direction.

The woman got up and moved close to the bus driver for protection.

"Stupid spreenie," I said from between clenched teeth.

"Stop muttering," Eleni said, obviously aware of the other people around us, all of whom had tense backs now.

The bell went off, indicating someone wanted to get off.

The driver pulled over to the curb and opened the doors, but nobody stood to leave.

The driver closed the doors and pulled the bus back into traffic.

A few seconds later, the bell went off once more.

Again the driver stopped, even though, again, no one was standing.

The driver said, "Whoever's messing with the bell, if I catch you at it, I'm throwing you off."

I held the lens up to my eye. I didn't see Larry, but I caught the gaze of the driver in the mirror, watching me.

I concentrated on looking innocent. Eleni suggested, "Maybe it's a malfunction."

The driver snorted and started the bus again.

And, just my luck, I suddenly recognized where we were. "I'm ringing the bell now," I announced, standing up to do it, to demonstrate that I had nothing to hide.

The driver sighed loud enough for us, halfway down the aisle, to hear, but he stopped and opened the door.

"Thank you," Eleni said brightly as she walked down the steps.

He took off again as soon as my feet hit the street, obviously not wanting to give us a chance to change our minds.

Despite the other people on the sidewalk, I put the lens to my eye and found Larry, once more sitting on Eleni's shoulder as though he'd never strayed. "I thought you wanted to do this," I said. "I thought this was serious business."

"Yes," Larry said to my first point, and "Yes," he said to the second.

"Then why couldn't you sit still for ten minutes?"

Bystanders, who thought the demented-farmhand-dressed girl was berating the presentable one, circled out of our way.

Larry said, "You might as well ask water not to be wet, or a maple not to shed its leaves in autumn. It's my very nature."

"Well, it's a *bad* nature," I said, and I put the lens back in my pocket so I wouldn't have to listen to his answer.

We walked the block from the office building

that would, in another fifty years or so, become my dentist's office, to the address of Westfall Nursing Home. I knew we were in trouble even before we got there. There were too many houses, not enough businesses.

"I think," I said with a sigh, "we need to check out a few backyards."

17

...And Yet So Far

I n an attempt not to look like a total freak to anyone who saw me, I wasn't keeping the lens at my eye.

But the next time I glanced through it, I saw Larry pulling someone's lawn sprinkler closer to the sidewalk so that—if the homeowner turned the water on without checking first—it would douse anybody walking by.

"Larry!" I said in the most menacing voice I could manage without raising my voice.

"What?" he asked in a tone of such total innocence, I would have known he was doing something wrong even if I *hadn't* seen him.

"The place I'm looking for isn't here."

"I can sense the gate nearby," he said, which was a relief in all sorts of ways. "I'd estimate behind that house there." He pointed two houses down.

I pointed, too, to let Eleni know.

But we hadn't taken more than one step into that yard when a voice yelled at us from the porch of the adjacent house: "You two!" It was an old lady's voice. A cranky old lady's voice. Without the lens, I was lucky I could see the porch, and I didn't want to raise the lens to my eye and risk looking like a pirate with a spyglass. "Yes, you two: you, with the blue dress, and the other one—the scruffy girl or effeminate boy—with her."

Boy? Well, that was certainly endearing, wasn't it?

She demanded, "Get off my lawn."

I didn't point out that, actually, we were on her neighbor's lawn. Instead, I said, "Ahhm..."

Luckily, Eleni was better with words. "What absolutely gorgeous begonias!" she exclaimed. "We just wanted to take a closer look."

"Don't you pick them!" the old lady said. "First, you'll be picking their begonias, then you'll be after my peonies."

"No," Eleni assured her, "neither. Just admiring."

"Well, admire from the sidewalk," the woman commanded.

I got back on the sidewalk and resumed walking away. I said dismissively, "Aww, they're probably all full of ants, anyway." Not exactly a way to make peace, but—come on!—she should have seen I do *not* look like a boy, even if I *was* wearing pants.

Eleni joined me and we strolled right on past the house where Larry had guessed the gate was likely to be. Then we stopped at the next house to sniff at the roses in a bush just a step or two into the yard. I put the lens to my eye and casually glanced back to check if the old lady was still watching.

Oh yeah: She was standing by the rail of the porch, her arms folded over her chest, and she was scowling directly at us.

"We'll have to go around the back of the block," I told Eleni.

Luckily, there were no paranoid-about-someone-stealing-their-flowers neighbors on the other street. I hoped our nosy lady hadn't moved to her back porch.

We cut through one yard, then had to detour around some laundry lines.

Larry plucked a sock off the line and started eating it.

"Stop it," I hissed at him.

"What?" he said. "I'm hungry. This is what spreenies eat: freshly laundered socks."

It explained a lot.

We had to squeeze through a hedge to avoid a fence. But when I put the lens to my eye, I saw the elven gate. "There it—"

Eleni yelped. Probably Larry did, too, but I couldn't hear him because a dog started barking. A dog that looked like a cross between a German shepherd and a grizzly bear. A dog that threw itself against the flimsy fence that was all that separated us from him. He was barking fiercely, like he was saying in dog-talk, "Fresh meat! Fresh meat! Fresh meat!"

We backed away from the fence—we didn't want that yard anyway, but the one that backed up to it, which was where the gate was. But like the nosy, crabby woman who suspected us of being flower thieves, that didn't satisfy the dog's territorial instincts.

"Nice doggy," Eleni said in a soothing voice. "Nice doggy."

She didn't convince any of us.

"My, what a fierce temper that dog has," Larry said. He'd been startled enough to drop what was left of the sock, and he was hovering anxiously behind me, keeping me between him and the dog's temper.

"Dogs can see spreenies?" I guessed.

"Oh yeah."

And eat them, too, I was willing to bet from Larry's edginess.

The dog was still barking and I was sure someone was going to come out to investigate and we were going to be stopped short just moments before we would have had success.

"Which direction does the gate work?" I asked Larry.

"Front to back. We need to all hold hands to make sure Eleni doesn't get left behind. My, what big teeth that dog has."

I could leave Eleni behind? Thank you for that information, Larry. After all, it was for her own good.

I had to turn around to face the gate. It looked just the same as ever, appearing to lead through to nothing more interesting than the neighbor's hydrangea bush, but I stepped toward it, trusting it would bring me to Kazaran Dahaani.

"My," Larry said, "what long legs that dog has."

"Larry," I couldn't help delaying to point out, "you're sounding like Little Red Riding Hood."

"No," Larry said, "I mean: *What long legs he has.*"

The hysterical twang of his voice made me glance over my shoulder just as the dog cleared the fence.

Eleni squealed in terror as the animal charged us.

I couldn't leave her behind with that vicious dog.

I grabbed her hand.

Larry caught hold of my hair.

And we all fell through the gate together.

18

Of Course More Complications

I ran smack into something.

Escaping through the archway, my only concern had been to avoid becoming kibble specially formulated for... well, whatever comes after *large* dogs. *Humongous, snarling, slobbering, can-eat-small-children-in-a-single-bite dogs?* Whatever. I'd been concentrating on not becoming any creature's lunch. With one hand, I was holding the lens to my eye so I could see; with the other, I was pulling my grandmother along behind me; and all the while I could still hear the furious barking. And I was hoping that was some sort of acoustical illusion of passing between worlds—because the quality of the light had changed, and I knew I had crossed over to Kazaran Dahaani. As all of this was going on—*pow!*—something and I collided.

Because of my panic, the image of what I'd run into didn't immediately make it from my retina to that part of my brain that makes sense of visual input. I had an impression of pale limbs, sparkles, and a flash of red before I went sprawling onto the ground, landing on someone, still dragging Eleni with me.

In Kazaran Dahaani, I didn't need glasses to see, which was good because I'd dropped the lens upon impact. From my position on the ground, I could clearly make out the fur on the rump of the dog as it leaped overhead to avoid the obstacle formed by Eleni and me and whoever we'd mowed down. I was aware of the dog skidding to a dusty stop on the path beyond us, then doing an about-face, and curling its doggy lips into a snarl directed—I was certain—at my throat. And I could hear a girl's high-pitched, hysterical screaming. Wasn't me, wasn't Eleni, wasn't the person with whom we'd collided.

Oh. That was okay then; it was just Larry. He was hovering in the air out of dog-jaw reach, his hands fluttering almost as fast as his iridescent wings. All of that registered before I caught sight of the strappy sandal of the person I'd run down. Then I saw the

sparkly skirt. Then the red spaghetti-strap top, re-
vealing more of a bony, age-spotted chest than anyone should ever have to see.

I'd run into Tiffanie Mills.

As *her* brain suddenly caught up with *her* retinas
and she recognized me, her eyes widened, sending a
whole mass of wrinkles up into her hairline—because
here in Kazaran Dahaani, Tiffanie was in Ugly Mode.

I was tempted to scream right along with Larry,
though the good news was that it didn't really make
any difference what evil Tiffanie had planned for me:
We had three sets of arms and legs entangled on the
ground, and there was no way we could sort them all
out before the dog would be feasting on our entrails.
In fact, even as I thought that, the dog leaped at us.

"*Stop!*" Tiffanie commanded, managing to get
her arm free and her hand held up like a traffic cop.

The dog stopped.

Midair.

Frozen, like a life-sized photo of an action shot,
drops of spittle not attached to anything but suspended in the sunlight.

Larry, unwilling to witness our death-by-canine
destruction, had fled somewhere between the time
the dog's paws left the ground and before its movement—and its barking—had been magically stilled.

In the sudden silence, Tiffanie said, "Don't you give me any of that 'Just protecting myself' nonsense," which seemed an incredibly odd thing to say, until I noticed her shaking her finger at the dog, like a stern kindergarten teacher. "I'm guessing you've been bullied yourself, but that doesn't give you the right to bully others. I'm going to let you down now, but you behave yourself."

The dog lowered to the ground, like a helicopter landing, which apparently unfroze him. He gave a menacing growl, and Tiffanie said, "Don't you take that tone with me. Just tell me what happened."

The dog barked, but though it went on and on, it wasn't that deep-throated I'm-about-to-eat-you sound.

While Tiffanie listened, I pulled my left arm out from under her and my right leg out from under Eleni.

Eleni, I was amazed to see, was looking as though she'd just opened a door to find the Land of Oz on the other side. Which, I guess, she sort of had—a demented, cutthroat, Stephen King version of Oz. I motioned for her to pull her dress back down over her knees, even though it wasn't anywhere near as high up the leg as Tiffanie's. I guess I'd already spent too much time in the 1950s.

"Yes," Tiffanie was saying to the dog, and "Go on," still giving that impression of a firm but kindly primary schoolteacher—or a psychotherapist—and "How do you think that made them feel?"

The dog hung its head in shame.

"Exactly," Tiffanie said. "Making others feel small and frightened doesn't do anything to make you feel better about yourself."

The dog gave a doggy whine.

"I understand," Tiffanie said, "but that only makes you just like the dogs that picked on you when you were small. Is that what you want to be?"

More barking, whining, and growling, and Tiffanie nodded. "Yes," she said. "I think that's a much better idea. Now please excuse me a minute." Still sitting on the ground, she turned and faced me, her skinny, age-spotted hand on her hip. All sympathetic gentleness was gone. "What are *you* doing here?" she demanded.

Despite all the time I'd had to come up with a reasonable explanation in case she asked this most obvious of questions, all I could come up with was "Ahmm..."

Eleni extended her hand for a handshake and said, "You must be Tiffanie. Hi, my name is Eleni." How could anyone resist that smile?

Tiffanie glowered at her, then demanded of me, "What have you gone and done?"

"I haven't done anything," I protested.

"Where did you get those glasses you had back there, and what have you done with them, and why are you following me?"

"Ahmm...," I said again, but I was glancing around on the ground, trying to find that dropped lens.

I spotted it a second after Eleni did.

Tiffanie spotted it a second after I did.

Just as Eleni leaned forward and picked it up, Tiffanie caught hold of her wrist.

"Don't you hurt my—" I don't know if it would have made any difference if my grandmother learned about how many years separated us, but I couldn't bring myself to call someone who looked only a year or so older than me "grandmother," so I finished with "ancestor."

I could tell from the look Eleni gave me that she didn't much appreciate my word choice. She said to Tiffanie, sounding more intent on making a point to me than to Tiffanie, "Yeah, and don't you hurt my *descendant*."

But Tiffanie didn't let herself get distracted. She shook Eleni's wrist, and my grandmother's grip jostled loose. Tiffanie snatched the lens up and demanded, "Where's the other one?"

I figured the truth couldn't get me into any more trouble. "Road debris back in 1950-something-or-other."

"Three," Eleni said.

Tiffanie examined the lens, which was scratched from its adventures and had a chip out of the upper corner where the frame had broken away. She looked at the two of us again, and must have decided to believe us. Or maybe she just decided it was time to move on to the next question. "Where did you get the glasses?"

"Isn't it *your* turn to answer one of *our* questions?" I asked.

"Probably," Tiffanie said. "My turn again: Where did you get the glasses?"

"I found them," I said, then got in a question of my own: "What are you doing going to James Fenimore Cooper High, pretending to be just one of the kids?"

Tiffanie ignored that. She said, "'I found them' is hardly a complete answer."

"I found them in my front yard yesterday evening," I snapped. "I don't know where they came from or how they got there."

"Liar," Tiffanie snarled.

Eleni jumped in to defend me. "Jeannette isn't a liar."

"Jeannette?" Tiffanie repeated with a smirk.

I figured my credibility was too badly damaged for her to believe Eleni had given me that name, so I didn't even bother.

Tiffanie asked, "So why are you and *Jeannette* following me?"

"We weren't following you," Eleni said. Her voice was calm and quiet, evidence of a reasonable demeanor, a frame of mind both Tiffanie and I were having trouble maintaining. "We all came through the gate just a few seconds after you, but we came from a different starting point." She indicated herself in her gauzy-but-still-covering-everything-up 1950s summer dress, then gestured to Tiffanie in her skimpy, leave-little-to-the-imagination outfit. In fact, it left even less than usual to the imagination, being all askew from our collision. Eleni added, "If we had been following you, you certainly would have heard us, especially the dog."

This made so much sense, Tiffanie couldn't ignore it.

Even the dog gave a short yip to signify agreement.

Tiffanie snorted, then asked, "So why are you here?"

"No," Eleni said in that cool, poised voice of hers, "it's definitely your turn now. Answer Jeannette's question about why you're going to her school."

How did she manage that tone? I needed to practice that. All I could do was nod for emphasis—very like a three-year-old.

Tiffanie snapped, "Well, I'm certainly not jeopardizing two distinct worlds."

"Could you please be more specific?" Eleni asked.

"To have fun," Tiffanie said. "To look good and be popular. For a change."

"Oh," I said, feeling small. Doesn't matter what world you come from: Ugly is ugly, and Tiffanie must have had a difficult time with her real appearance.

Eleni nudged me with her elbow. "You see?" she said, oozing self-satisfaction.

I threw one of her own sayings back at my grandmother, which she had used on me when I was ten and she'd caught me gloating about something or other: "Nice people don't say, 'I told you so.'"

Eleni raised her eyebrows, perhaps surprised to hear me use one of her pet phrases that, as far as she knew, she'd never used in front of me.

Or, more likely, I realized with sudden horror, she

NOW YOU SEE IT . . .

herself had never yet spoken this sentiment but was thinking it was a great one to adopt. Had my saying it to her just now been the reason she'd say it to me later in her life but earlier in mine?

That kind of thinking was bound to give me a headache.

Tiffanie asked, emphasizing every single word: "So . . . what . . . are . . . you . . . doing . . . in . . . *my* . . . world?"

"We're here to rescue Julian," Eleni said.

Tiffanie's voice dripped skepticism. "From what?"

"Bear . . ." I rummaged around in my brain for the name Larry had used for Julian's abductor. "Bear Tooth? Bare Naked? . . ."

While Eleni winced at my language, Tiffanie asked in a voice of horror, "Berrech?"

"Something like that," I agreed.

Tiffanie repeated, to make sure she had it right: "Berrech has captured Julian?"

"Yeah, Berrech and four other guys. Elves."

"How long ago?"

I glanced at my wristwatch. "Almost two hours."

"Don't mess with me," Tiffanie warned. "We were in school two hours ago."

"Time flies when you're having fun." I held out my wrist for her to see my watch, which indicated it was getting close to five. My mother would definitely be at the nursing home by now, and wondering where I was.

Tiffanie made an impatient brushing-away gesture. "Not how long has it been since you saw him," she said. "How long has it been *here*?"

I gave the only appropriate response: "Huh?"

Eleni caught on faster. "Time didn't move here in Kazaran Dahaani while Jeannette was with me?"

Tiffanie said, "Well, obviously time doesn't *stop* here while *you personally* are not paying attention, but no matter how much time you spend away, you always come back to the same time you left from. How long has it been *here*?"

"Fifteen minutes?" I guessed.

Had it really been only fifteen minutes? I'd assumed that—while I'd been back in the 1950s, semi-successfully dodging cars and totally unsuccessfully dodging Eleni's questions—Berrech and his bully elves had had more than enough time to do whatever they wanted to Julian. I'd been sure it was too late to help him, anyway. I wouldn't have been so intent on leaving Eleni behind and losing Larry if I'd realized how little time had actually passed.

Of course, that was easy to say now that I had people with expectations of me—and no way to get out without *proving* to them and to myself that I was a cowardly weasel.

Tiffanie got to her feet, looking ready to do the hundred-yard dash.

"Excuse me," Eleni said, "but shouldn't we have a plan?"

19

History and Bribes

No time!" Tiffanie said. "Which way did they take him?"

Eleni knocked my hand down as I pointed, and said, "First we need to—" but it was too late. Tiffanie was on her feet and running down the path.

The dog, after hesitating a moment, followed.

"*Stop* her," Eleni commanded me. "I can't run in these heels."

"Yeah, but...," I started to say, thinking, *Tiffanie has everything under control. We can go home.*

"Stop her!" Eleni gave me a shove even as she slipped off her high heels, and started running, too.

I could abandon Tiffanie; I could abandon Julian; but—even if we hadn't been related—I couldn't abandon Eleni. She kept expecting the best of me, and I kept thinking it would be nice to be the person she thought I was.

I quickly passed her and started closing in on Tiffanie. Tiffanie sure was fast for an old crone who jiggled and bounced so much I was sure she was going to hurt herself. "Tiffanie!" I called. "You can't do this all alone!"

The dog yipped, evidently pointing out she *wasn't* all alone.

Tiffanie stopped, panting hard and pressing her hand to her side. She pulled the hem of her skimpy top down to cover her old-lady belly button.

Eleni caught up. "Can you do that thing you do?" she asked. "To those elves? Like you did with the dog?"

"No," Tiffanie had to admit. "Maybe one, but certainly not all at once—elves are hard to bespell." Looking like it hurt her to accept our help, she asked, "All right—what's your plan?"

"Gosh, I don't have a plan," Eleni admitted. "I don't know enough about the situation."

Tiffanie growled in frustration but didn't start running again, which probably had more to do with her age than Eleni's persuasive abilities.

"Who are these other elves?" Eleni asked. "Why have they taken Julian?"

"All right," Tiffanie said, still breathing heavily, "the history lesson in brief: Julian's father is Nivyn the king. Berrech is the son of King Nivyn's brother, Vediss. Vediss was the elder, but when the old king, their father, was dying, he knew Vediss did not have the disposition to be a wise ruler, and he named Nivyn his successor."

We were already beyond my idea of *brief*.

Tiffanie continued, "It's hard to tell if Vediss was as comfortable with that decision as he seemed, but for certain Berrech feels an injustice was done. Whatever King Nivyn says, Berrech will argue for the opposite."

"That's a lot of names to keep straight," I complained when she stopped for a breath.

"Don't talk to me about names," she snapped, and I considered myself lucky that she didn't take the opportunity to call me "Wendy."

"Where this affects you two, Eleni and *Jeannette,* is in the king's policy toward humans. The old king had declared humans too volatile a species and he closed the gates *his* father's father had built when humans and elves shared each other's worlds. Kazaran Dahaani was cut off from Earth for many generations of humankind."

I wanted to ask her about the generations of elfkind, but she didn't give me a chance.

"King Nivyn believes humans are a worthwhile species, and that elves and humans have much to offer one another despite their differences, and so he has reopened the gates, and has even sent his son into the human world to learn more of it. Being opposed to all the king stands for, Berrech, therefore, believes humans are worse than dangerous: They are careless of their own world, and Berrech feels that with their advancing technology they will destroy both their world and ours. He wants to rid Earth of humans. Do you see why this is serious?"

It would be hard not to.

Eleni asked, "Where do these glasses Jeannette found come in?"

Tiffanie opened her hand. She was still holding the one remaining lens. "I don't know what this is. I've never seen anything like it: something that strips away the supernatural. I can sense magic in it—but I can't detect any spell."

"Who could have made them?" Eleni pressed. "And why?"

"I have no idea *who*," Tiffanie said. "*Why* would seem to be to allow someone to find those of us from Kazaran Dahaani who have gone to Earth, to see beyond the glamours we have cast to pass unnoticed among you."

"And who would that benefit?" Eleni asked, though she could guess as well as I could.

"Berrech," Tiffanie said. "Berrech could use that to track us down. To find Julian, certainly, before you led the poor boy right into his hands."

How was I to know?

She gave me a hard look. "He was just trying to *talk* to you," she said in an accusing tone. "When neither of you came out of that nursing home, I went in and found you'd caused an uproar running all over the garden and then disappearing. I figured you must have gone through the gate." She shook her head at my foolishness.

"I didn't know he wasn't going to hurt me," I protested.

Tiffanie didn't point out that I was whining. Apparently she was still thinking about those glasses. "Berrech could also use them to find the rest of us. I suppose he could have arranged for bad things to happen to us, bad things he could blame on the humans, to sway public opinion his way: proof that humans are dangerous to our kind and should be destroyed."

"I didn't know," I muttered again.

Eleni patted my shoulder reassuringly. She said, "So, someone sympathetic to Berrech's cause made the glasses . . . And then what? Accidentally dropped them on Jeannette's front lawn? That would be a happy coincidence for the good guys."

"Yeah," Tiffanie said, "lost stuff, stuff showing up—if I didn't know better, I'd say a spreenie was involved in that."

"*Larry,*" Eleni and I said simultaneously.

Tiffanie eyed us suspiciously. "Who's Larry?"

"A little blue annoyance factory," I explained. Brave soul that he was, he'd deserted us when it looked as though we were about to be dismembered. But after he'd stuck with me back in 1953, after he'd all but dragged us back here, it was hard to believe he'd gone far. "Larry!" I shouted. "Larry, you get your miserable blue butt out here!"

Eleni joined in, once again in a tone that displayed no anger: "Larry? Larry, where are you?"

The dog barked.

Tiffanie put her hands on her hips and glowered in all directions.

Well, I couldn't blame Larry for not wanting to come out to *that* face. We needed to entice him out, and while I was wondering how to do that, I remembered his snacking on that sock hanging from the clothesline. Did spreenies only like freshly laundered socks?

I threw myself down on the ground, unlaced my sneaker, and whipped off my sock. "A sock, Larry." I waved it in the air. "A nice, warm"—would *sweaty* be a good or bad adjective as far as he was concerned?—"mmm, tasty sock."

It was a silly plan.

But it worked.

Larry came darting out from the branches of a nearby tree and snatched the sock out of my hand.

"You survived," he said, hovering just out of my reach. "How nice for you." He crammed the sock into his mouth.

Though he seemed preoccupied with his... treat...when Tiffanie made a grab for him, he shot a couple feet higher in the air.

Eleni asked, "Where did you get the glasses, Larry?"

Munching happily away, Larry mumbled something that sounded like...

"*Vediss?*" Tiffanie squealed.

"Where, exactly?" Eleni asked.

"Give me one of your stockings, sweetie," Larry said to her, still chewing his wad of sock, "and I'll tell you."

"You disgusting little pervert," I said.

"Yes," Larry cooed, "but that's why you love me."

"I hate you," I corrected him, but Eleni was already sitting on the ground taking off a stocking. I shooed him away when he zoomed in trying to catch a better look.

Eleni dangled the stocking. "Where?" she asked.

"There's a cave, near Dragons' Cove. Give me a kiss, and I'll tell you *how* they work."

"I'm dying here," I groaned in protest.

But Eleni puckered her lips.

Larry swooped in, grabbed the stocking—which, I was glad to see, showed he had his priorities in the right place: food before sexual harassment—and momentarily brushed his itty-bitty lips against hers.

Tiffanie tried her stop-action spell on him, but he was too quick, darting hummingbird-fashion, there one second, somewhere else the next.

"Silly, silly girls," he called all of us. "The lenses are magical, but they haven't been bespelled."

"Just *talk,* spreenie," Tiffanie commanded.

"Been going to high school for almost twenty years now," he jeered at her, "and you still don't know anything."

"Larry," Eleni wheedled, "you promised you'd explain."

"How is glass made?" Larry asked.

Tiffanie was in a bad mood from his insult, and she shot back, "Who cares?"

"In a glass factory," I guessed.

"With sand," Eleni said.

"A prize for the pretty lady!" Larry said, pointing at Eleni. "And what does Dragons' Cove have plenty of?"

"Sand?" Eleni asked.

"A wonderful guess!" Larry cheered. "And...," he prompted.

"Dragons?"

"Hooray!" Larry said, and jammed the whole stocking into his mouth.

It was Tiffanie who put it all together: "Generations of dragons have gone to Dragons' Cove to lay their eggs. The sand there must have a high dragon-shell content. So glass lenses made with that sand might have magical properties."

Larry made an expansive gesture with this arms. "Who says you're as dumb as you look?" he asked.

Tiffanie tried again to stop him in his tracks.

"Course," he added, having bobbed away, "I would have told you even without the stocking or the kiss. I don't like Berrech. And his socks taste even sweatier than yours," he told me.

Eleni, who'd suddenly caught on that she'd been kissed by someone who'd just eaten a sweaty sock, rubbed the back of her hand across her mouth.

I said, "So now, at least, we know where Berrech is probably taking Julian."

Tiffanie considered, wanting—I suspect—to call me an idiot who was *always* wrong.

"'Cause," I explained, "would Berrech just take Julian back to the old Berrech homestead in the middle of Elf Village or wherever, and hold him prisoner there in the hopes that none of the neighbors would notice? Or would he take him to the cave his father's conducting secret experiments at?"

Larry blew a big, wet kiss in my direction.

"This is beginning to sound like a plan," Tiffanie grudgingly agreed.

20

The Fellowship of the Lens

Our plan, such as it was, was to hurry—now that we had done such a good job of delaying Tiffanie. But at least now we knew where Berrech was taking Julian, so Tiffanie wouldn't lose time trying to track them. The reason we were in a rush was because—for now—the good guys (we assumed that was us) equaled the bad guys (Berrech and his four hench-elves). The odds would only get worse once they reached the cave, where Berrech's dad, Vediss, was likely to be, maybe with even more supporters.

Five or six trained warrior elves versus five of us: me (Little Miss Always-Chosen-Last-in-Team-Sports),

Eleni (Miss Innocent of 1953), Tiffanie (who, no matter what she looked like when she fixed herself up, without magic looked about a hundred years beyond prime), Larry (whose bravery in the face of danger we'd witnessed when the dog was set on teaching us the difference between his territory and the rest of the world), and the dog.

Though the dog could understand human speech, he only spoke Dog; and Tiffanie, it turned out, was the only one among us who was fluent in Dog. No big surprise there. She told us that he told her his name was Brave Heart.

"Funny," I said, "you don't look like Mel Gibson."

Tiffanie, the only one who caught my reference, didn't think it was funny.

Larry asked, "What if we run into a group of elves and there's no way of knowing whether they're part of Berrech's faction or the king's?"

Tiffanie said, "Berrech doesn't have that many supporters."

I wondered how many was "not that many," but I didn't ask just in case I didn't like the answer.

Larry said, "But it might be dangerous to assume anybody we run into is with the king."

"We're not likely to run into anyone," Tiffanie told him. "Dragons' Cove is not that far."

"But *what if*?" Larry insisted. "What if we *do* meet up with some elves with their songs and their silver bells and their bet-you-can't-guess-what-I'm-thinking faces, and their swords and their bows and arrows and their magical trinkets?"

Tiffanie had no more patience for reassuring him, but Eleni asked, "Why are you asking?"

"Because," Larry said, "there's a group of elves heading this way now."

Once he said it, I could hear them—a snatch of song, the tinkling of silver bells—though the curve of the path hid them for the moment from our sight: a large number from the sound of them, talking and laughing among themselves.

Eleni said, "We look so strange, we're bound to attract attention and questions."

My inclination was to run and hide, but nobody asked me.

"All right," Tiffanie said, "I'm going to cast a glamour over all of us, make the three of us look like elf shepherdesses. And Brave Heart, I'll make you look like a sheep. Whatever you do, don't bark."

I was about to point out that her look-like-a-cheerleader spell wasn't working in Kazaran Dahaani, but apparently she knew that and used a different spell. The sensation was like being licked all over by a cat: somewhere between ticklish and irritating.

In less time than it takes to say, Eleni and I became very blond and willowy, which—hey!—had long been a goal in my life. Now we were both wearing dresses made of an incredibly soft, fluttery material: mine in a heathery green, Eleni's a slightly more bluish shade.

As gorgeous as Eleni looked and I felt, Tiffanie had made herself look considerably more gorgeous, with hair that went on and on, and her gown was sunset pink, with iridescent threads at the neckline.

Brave Heart looked like a sheep, except he was sitting on the path, scratching behind his ear in a very doglike manner.

The elves were just beyond the bend.

"Hey!" Larry said. "Hey! What about me?"

"What?" Tiffanie asked softly, so as not to let the elves hear.

"You said you were going to cast a glamour. You said, 'on all of you.' Where's my disguise?"

"You don't need one. Spreenies belong here. Or you can just..." She waved her hand treetop-ward.

"I want a disguise."

"Stop making a scene."

"I want—"

Tiffanie made an abrupt gesture, then ordered from between clenched teeth, "Get on a tree branch *now*"—because her magic had made Larry take on the shape of a tree toad.

"Thanks a lot," he grumbled, just as the party of twelve or fifteen elves came into sight.

I could see right away that the spell only disguised us because otherwise Larry would have plummeted to the ground like...well, like a tree toad who'd been caught in midair. Instead, he must have flapped his little wings which had become invisible to us, and he hid himself, still grumbling, among the leaves of the trees.

Fortunately, the elves didn't notice him.

Unfortunately, the elves did notice us—which, I guess, was pretty much unavoidable with us right there in the middle of their path; but, anyway, we'd taken our magical precaution.

Fortunately, they seemed a social group rather than a military troop, male and female elves in clothes too fluttery and delicate to be anything besides party clothes, with flower wreaths in their hair, and bells sewn into their garments and tied at their wrists and ankles, and carrying baskets of flowers and fruit as though they were on their way to a picnic.

Unfortunately, they were so social that they decided to stop to chat with us.

Fortunately, they—or at least the males in the group—seemed most interested in the extremely gorgeous Tiffanie.

Unfortunately—

Oh, forget that. Things looked okay for the moment, but always with the possibility of turning bad.

"Well met, shepherd lasses!" they greeted us. "Come, join us in celebrating the day."

They crowded around us—well, mostly Tiffanie—and begged, "Please!" and "Come!" and "How could we be festive without you?"

"No, no," Tiffanie told them, "thank you for the kind invitation, but my sisters and I must be heading home."

"Oh, that is so disappointing!" one of the more persistent males said. "Still, if you don't have time to join us for a meal on the greensward, at least join us for a song."

"Or let us braid flowers into your hair," another enterprising elf said, taking some flowers from the basket he carried. He started to twine them in Tiffanie's extravagant hair, though I heard him murmur, "Your hair looks so lush, but feels...so much finer and more delicate."

One of the females started a song that was composed almost entirely of notes that—if they went any higher—would have been beyond human hearing.

They must have been on the threshold of hurting Brave Heart's ears, for he started whining.

"Listen, listen," the elves cried, laughing, their voices as clear as the bells they wore. "The girls' sheep is trying to sing along with Sylvianna!"

Which, of course, the elf girl Sylvianna took as encouragement to put even more high-note flourishes into her song.

Tiffanie rested her hand on Brave Heart's head, to calm him.

Not working, I could tell. Things were about to go seriously wrong. I could see the wool on Brave Heart's haunches bristle.

He was about to bark at the euphonious Sylvianna—if not take a bite out of her: either of which was decidedly an unsheeplike reaction.

I prepared to grab Eleni's hand and run for the gate. If we passed through back into our world with Tiffanie's spell on us, would we continue to look this way? Good news for me. But for my grandmother, maybe not. She had already been attractive, but now she was attractive in a totally different way. Would she and my grandfather still end up marrying if she looked this way? I took a step toward her and realized only by the tug on my hair that one of the elves was busy weaving daisies into my hair, too.

"Ow!" Sylvianna stopped singing and put her hand to the back of her neck.

"What?" people asked her.

"I think it was an acorn," she said. "That was the second one to land on my head."

"It's too early for acorns to be falling," her friends told her.

But sure enough, we could all see two green acorns on the path.

"One would almost suspect there were spreenies about," someone observed.

The elves peered into the trees, while Tiffanie continued to pat Brave Heart's head. "Down," she murmured, probably meaning "Calm down," but he sat. Tiffanie tugged on the wool on the back of his neck to get him to stand before anyone else noticed.

The elves were preoccupied looking for a spreenie.

"No," one of them finally announced, "no spreenies. All I see is that ugly tree toad."

Eleni said, "I hear it's been a bad year for tree toads. They've gotten extremely bold."

The elves had short attention spans. They turned back to Tiffanie and Brave Heart. I saw the tree toad pluck another acorn and lob it at the back of the head of the elf who'd called him ugly, but luckily the elf couldn't tell where it had come from and looked directly up rather than behind him.

At least Sylvianna had been distracted from singing. "What's your sheep's name?" she asked, crouching in front of Brave Heart to peer into his face.

"Brave—" Tiffanie started, then apparently realizing Brave Heart wasn't an appropriate name for a sheep, finished, "Fluffy."

"Brave Fluffy," the elf girl cried, delighted. She switched to baby talk. "My, aren't you just the sweetest little thing!"

Brave Heart bared his teeth at her, but as they only looked like sheep teeth, the girl didn't take alarm.

"Join us," the elves continued to urge. "It will be so much fun." They tugged on our arms. Tiffanie, Eleni, and I dug our heels into the ground. The guys tugging on me and Eleni picked up the subtle nuance that we didn't want to go. The two trying to entice Tiffanie were more stubborn.

Brave Heart growled at them.

Sylvianna—who'd been nose to nose with him— scrambled to her feet in alarm, but the males just wouldn't give up.

Brave Heart decided it was time to stake out his territory. I saw him check out the leg of the nearest elf. Then he lifted his own leg, and peed.

It was a real conversation-stopper.

"Really," Eleni said, prying loose the fingers of one of the elves who'd been laughing and holding on to Tiffanie's wrists, "Fluffy gets very anxious when away from the other sheep for too long."

The elves finally took the hint. Even the one who'd been trying to put flowers into Tiffanie's hair. They kept falling out, anyway.

"Well, if you're sure...," one of the female elves said. In any case, she'd probably worked out that if we joined them, the girls would outnumber the guys. Actually, with Tiffanie among them, there wouldn't be any leftover guys no matter how few girls there were.

"Have a good picnic," I said. I'd been just about useless through the entire incident, and I began waving even though they weren't moving yet.

"Good-bye," they told us. "Farewell."

We watched, smiling and waving as they continued down the path, until they disappeared around another bend. One of them took up a song again, and we waited until their voices faded.

So that was one crisis out of the way. I could only hope I'd be more useful next time.

21

The Bluebird of Unhappiness

W e'd better stay disguised, don't you think?" Eleni asked Tiffanie. "In case we run into any other people?"

I wanted to add, *You might want to pick a look that's less attention grabbing,* but I didn't have a chance.

Eleni continued, "Unless keeping up the spell tires you or weakens you."

I would have thought of that first part, eventually, but never the last part, proving yet again how much smarter than me my grandmother was. And more considerate. Without even having to stop to think about it.

But, for all that, Tiffanie made a dismissive gesture. "Glamours don't take that much power."

NOW YOU SEE IT . . .

"Yeah, speaking of glamours"—Larry hovered in front of her face, closer than he needed to be—"I don't want to be disguised as a toad."

You'd have thought a big tough dog like Brave Heart would have resented looking like a sheep. But Brave Heart seemed to have become attached to Tiffanie despite his woolly state, and he barked at Larry for giving Tiffanie a hard time.

A barking sheep. A barking sheep barking at a levitating toad. It's the kind of image that could well trigger serious mental problems later in my life.

Tiffanie asked Larry, "What do you want to look like? Vole? Shrew? *Rat?*"

"How about something that *flies,* you lackwit," he suggested, "seeing as how that's how I travel and the whole purpose of these so-called disguises is so that we can pass without attracting attention?"

"A bird," Eleni suggested brightly, as though it had never occurred to her that that was obvious and that Tiffanie was being intentionally obtuse.

"The Bluebird of Unhappiness," I suggested. "The Bluebird of Downright Dysfunction."

"Oh, I am *so* amused," Larry said. To Tiffanie he said, "How about an eagle?"

"You're too small to be an eagle," Tiffanie said. "The spell would have to extend way beyond your actual parameters." She moved her hands from roughly five inches apart—approximately Larry-sized—to two or three feet apart, to demonstrate an eagle's wingspan.

"Not a powerful enough witch to do it?" Larry taunted.

"I am tempted to leave you this way forever," Tiffanie threatened, but she flicked her fingers at him, and the toad shifted to a little bird that looked sort of like a small gray cardinal.

"What am I?" Larry asked, twisting in midair, trying to catch a look at his backside.

"Tufted titmouse," Tiffanie said, "for the pure joy of the silliness of the name." Then she was all business: "Come on, let's go. We've wasted a lot of time, and Julian is in danger."

We started walking, two pretty elven shepherd-esses, one drop-dead-gorgeous elven shepherdess, and a sheep with a tendency to sniff at the edge of the path and to chase after butterflies. Followed by a tufted tit-mouse that grumbled and criticized all the way.

"So," I said, trying to be sensible and logical, thinking ahead, planning...like my grandmother. "Dragons' Cove..."

Eleni waited expectantly, while Tiffanie wore a pained expression that indicated she just knew I was about to say something worthless.

"Dragons' Cove," Larry repeated in a slow, dim tone, as though I'd just caught up to the conversation of fifteen minutes ago.

"So...," I said again. "Sand..."

Eleni nodded encouragingly.

"And dragon eggshells..." Hopefully, I finished, "But of course...no dragons?"

"Nooo," Larry said, "baby dragons grow on baby dragon bushes and are plucked by storks, then delivered to happy dragon mommies and daddies. No dragons involved. Nuh-uh. Rated PG. Definitely."

"Laying and hatching season is in early spring," Tiffanie assured me.

Just to be sure, I pressed on. "And dragons don't go to Dragons' Cove except then?"

"Sometimes," Larry said.

"Almost never," Tiffanie corrected him.

Almost. Great.

"Not to worry," Tiffanie assured us.

"Except—," Larry started.

Tiffanie had finally had enough of him. "Would you just stop instigating and shut up?"

Larry gave an aggrieved snort, flapping his little titmouse wing to his little titmouse breast.

"Zip it," Tiffanie ordered.

In the suddenly Larry-free silence, Eleni finally asked in her quiet voice, "Except...?"

Tiffanie sighed.

Eleni pretended she didn't notice. "Glass is made with sand and extreme heat."

Tiffanie sighed even louder. "Can't humans make glass without dragon-breath flame?"

"Well, sure," I started, "but—"

"That was a rhetorical question, honey," Tiffanie said. "There won't be any dragons, so let's just concentrate on getting there fast while Julian is still in one piece."

I could tell Eleni wasn't satisfied with Tiffanie's high-handed manner of rushing us, but she didn't say anything. She stopped, though, took off her shoe, and shook it as if to get out a stone.

I hung back, as did Larry, who obviously liked Eleni best of all of us. Tiffanie didn't wait, apparently figuring we could catch up, and Brave Heart stayed by her.

In a low voice, Eleni asked Larry, "Did you see any dragons while you were hanging around the cave watching Vediss make the lenses?"

Larry made a bunch of inarticulate noises, and motioned with the tip of his wing toward his beak. *Zip it,* Tiffanie had told him.

A fine time for him to choose to listen to any of us.

WE PASSED a pond and saw some elves at the far end, sitting on a raft with their feet cooling in the water, lazily drifting. They waved, and we waved back, but they were too far away to talk or to talk to, and fortunately they weren't interested enough in us to paddle their raft closer.

There were getting to be fewer and scrubbier trees, and in very short order the ground got rocky, then sandy, then I became aware of a noise that I recognized—though I'd never heard it before—as the roar of the sea.

We had reached Dragons' Cove.

Tiffanie threw herself down onto the ground behind a sand dune. "All right," she said once we'd all hunkered down and joined her, "we need to cause distractions to try to separate them. Now, there's at least five of them, and they have no reason to be wary of us at first, so maybe I can entice one to follow me, and we can get him out of the way."

I loved the way she glossed over that.

"Then I can make Brave Heart look like a wolf"—he pricked up his little sheep ears at that— "which might get one or two more of them to pursue him. That would leave two, and I could use what you called my 'stop-action' spell on one, and surely all of us together could overpower the last."

"I think you're making this sound too easy," I said.

Eleni said, "How about a reconnaissance mission?"

"Huh?" Tiffanie and I both asked.

"Larry, would you be willing to go into the cave ahead of us and let us know exactly what the setup is so there won't be any surprises?"

I expected Larry to make his can't-open-my-beak mumbling, but he didn't have the attention span to keep up any one single annoying action for very long. "Do I get a new disguise?" he asked.

From between clenched teeth, Tiffanie said, "Even if I could make you look like an eagle, an eagle could hardly slip unnoticed into the cave."

Larry pouted.

Eleni said, "How about a wren?"

"Boring," Larry told her.

"A wren is beautiful in an understated way," Eleni corrected him. "As well as being brave, and diligent, and noble."

I have no idea if she was making this up, but Larry bought it. "Okay," he said.

Before he could change his mind, Tiffanie turned him into a wren, which looked pretty drab to me, and he flew toward the shore.

We peeked our heads up over the sand dune and watched him fly into a hole in the bottom of a cliff that was near the water's edge.

We waited.

And waited.

And waited.

Until I was sure he'd been spotted and captured.

Then he came out again and flew back to where we were, which was more of a relief to me than it should have been.

He settled on top of Brave Heart's head. Brave Heart snapped, but couldn't get at him.

"Well," Larry said, "the bad news is that Vediss is with them, so that's one more than you counted on."

Now it was Tiffanie's turn to pout.

"What's the good news?" Eleni asked.

"There is no good news," Larry told her. "There's bad and there's worse." Despite his words, he was obviously pleased with himself. He gave a little victory dance in the air, waggling his tail, and trilled in a gloating singsong: "There's a dragon! There's a dragon! Shouldn't have told me to shut up! There's a dragon!"

22

Any Plan Is Better Than None—
Isn't It?

Well," Tiffanie said. "So there's a dragon. That really doesn't change anything."

"Ohh," I assured her, "I'm guessing it probably does—at least a little."

"No," Tiffanie argued, "we still have to rescue Julian." She looked ready to rush in alone if necessary.

I'm assuming I looked ready to let her, but I'm not sure. Yeah, yeah, he was the good guy, and the bad guys had it in for humans—I got all that—but that seemed a much less tangible danger than coming face-to-face with a dragon.

"Just," Eleni said calmly, "hold on. We all want to help Julian, but we won't be helping him if we fail because we didn't take a few moments to think this out."

Eleni's ability to think things out, to put things into perspective, could be simultaneously inspiring and annoying.

Tiffanie folded her arms over her chest, drumming her fingers, just barely containing—for the moment—the urge to be moving.

"All right," Eleni said, "Larry. What, exactly, did you see?"

"Dragon," Larry said. "Dragon, dragon, dragon. *Big* dragon." He nodded for emphasis, because his wings were so small that even extending them fully fell short of the impression he wanted to give. "Fire-breathing dragon." He made a noise which I presumed was supposed to be the sound of flame coming out from between dragon jaws, but as it came out of a wren's beak, that was only an educated guess.

"Just one dragon?" Eleni asked.

Just? I thought.

But I could see why she was asking. Even though he was using the singular *dragon,* he kept saying the word so often, it sounded like he was talking about a whole herd. Pack. Swarm. Flock. Whatever you call dragons when there's a whole mess of them.

"Just one." Larry made the combustible-breath sound again as though we needed a reminder. "He saw me," Larry said. "He tried to make wren fricassee out of me." Yet again he did his fire-breathing dragon impersonation. Still, his attitude seemed not so much frightened as exhilarated. I started suspecting he just liked making that sound of whooshing flame. He said, "I risked my life for you."

"Thank you," Eleni said, managing to avoid veering from briskness into sarcasm. She glanced over the crest of the sand dune and observed, "Luckily, he didn't follow you."

"No," Larry admitted, with perhaps a bit of the self-importance knocked out of him.

I wasn't as generous a person as my grandmother. *I* pointed out, "Couldn't have been *too* hungry."

Larry stamped his little bird foot on Brave Heart's woolly head.

Brave Heart growled.

"Spill it, Larry," Tiffanie ordered.

Larry fidgeted with his feet, like a toddler being forced to confess to some wrongdoing. He finally mumbled, "He was chained."

"Chained?" I repeated skeptically. "What kind of chain can hold a big, fire-breathing dragon?"

"Iron," Tiffanie said. "Iron binds those of us from Kazaran Dahaani."

"Ah," I said. "Why?"

"Just does."

Eleni had a better question. She asked, "So this dragon is being held prisoner?"

In his most insincere voice, Larry mumbled, "I was about to tell you."

Rather than argue, Eleni asked, "Are dragons intelligent?"

"Compared to what?" Tiffanie countered. She was looking straight at Larry. She added, "I don't know what the average IQ is for dragons. We don't go in for standardized testing much here in Kazaran Dahaani."

I admired how Eleni could keep calm despite Tiffanie's goading. She said, "I don't need to know if this dragon could be accepted at an Ivy League college. I need to know if it would realize that it was being rescued and cooperate in that rescue."

Trying not to sound contradictory-of-everything the way Tiffanie did, I still had to point out, "Like we don't have enough to worry about with rescuing Julian? Now you're developing a soft spot in your heart for captive dragons?"

Eleni sighed. "I'm not talking about an additional task. If we help the dragon, maybe the dragon will help us. *If* the dragon is intelligent enough not to make fricassee out of all of us."

Tiffanie was nodding, but then again, she would have agreed to anything to keep us moving. I asked, "So, like, how intelligent is 'intelligent'?"

"They can talk," Tiffanie said, then added with a malicious grin aimed directly at me, "though that's certainly not a sure indicator of intelligence." Before I could demonstrate *my* intelligence with a quick comeback, she added, "They can reason, remember, plan, plot, hold grudges. We can assume this dragon will be at least as intelligent as the majority of the people we go to school with."

I wasn't intelligent enough to be able to determine if she was praising dragons or slamming the student body at James Fenimore Cooper.

Larry said, "If you're looking for a volunteer to go in there and sweet-talk that dragon, I volunteer Tiffanie."

Tiffanie rebutted with, "Yeah, well, I volunteer you."

Eleni, the peacekeeper, told Larry, "Your size does make you the one most likely to pass undetected."

"No," I said.

Everyone turned to look at me.

"Come on," I explained, "could we really be sure the little blue perpetual-chaos machine wouldn't screw up?"

While Larry looked resentful, and Tiffanie looked thoughtful, and Brave Heart scratched an itch, Eleni clarified "screw up" for herself by asking, "You mean do something bad?"

"Yeah," I said. "Or stupid. Or he might kind of lose track of what he's supposed to be doing and wander off to do something else entirely."

Larry made a motion with his wing at his beak, which was probably the wren equivalent of thumbing his nose at me. "All right," he said, "if you think you can do so much better, then go ahead."

Surely it hadn't sounded as though *I'd* volunteered, had it?

"I never said that," I protested.

Eleni sided with me. "It's too dangerous for Jeannette," she said. "I'll go."

Which wasn't what I'd been hoping for, either. "How is it less dangerous for you than for me?"

For once Eleni didn't have a good answer. "Well," she said, stalling for time, then settled for "I'm older than you..."

Maybe by one year. I countered with, "Are you saying you're smarter and better able to handle the situation?"

"No," she said, then realized she'd cut away her best argument, and shifted to "Yes," then realized she'd just called me incompetent, so tried "I just don't want anything to happen to you."

"*Absolutely nothing* will happen to me if you get killed," I said. "In fact, I won't even get born." Afraid that if *I* said it, it would sound too sentimental, I muttered, "And I don't want anything to happen to you, either."

I was arguing to go into a cave with five nasty warrior elves and one-of-them's nasty father in order to ask for help from a fire-breathing dragon who might be intelligent but whose temper had to be short from having been kept a prisoner for who-knew-how-long? Maybe Tiffanie was right to disparage the intelligence of me and my friends at school.

But that was how we came up with our plan.

JULIAN, according to Larry, was being held in a cage in the back part of the cave, next to where the dragon was anchored by heavy chains fastened to a collar of iron around its neck. Vediss and his son, Berrech, were huddled over a workbench to the right of the cave entrance—we presumed trying to fashion a replacement pair of glasses that would allow Berrech to return to Earth to track down those from Kazaran Dahaani who were disguised as humans. At another table to the left, Berrech's four hench-elves were setting out food since it was—Larry pointed out in a piteous tone as though he hadn't been the only one among us to have eaten—dinnertime. I guess socks must be like Chinese takeout: twenty minutes later, you're hungry again.

"Are elves magical?" Eleni asked, which I thought was a reasonable question considering we were about to take them on, though not one I would have thought of. We should know if they were going to be able to throw magical spells at us, and couldn't assume Tiffanie would have told us.

But Tiffanie rolled her eyes. "Elves have magical artifacts, but they possess no magic themselves. That's why I had to cast a glamour over Julian when he went to school on Earth. Are we ready, or are we going to talk this to death?"

Bad choice of wording, as far as I was concerned.

We were as ready as we were likely to get.

The first part of the plan was for Tiffanie to go down to the shore the long way round, so as not to be seen if any of the elves glanced out the cave entrance.

We watched her go into the water, for which I had to give her credit, 'cause I'm assuming it had to be cold. In Tiffanie's case, besides being about a hundred years old, she didn't have an ounce of insulating fat on her. I've noticed that the skinnier a girl is, the more likely she is to complain that any body of water is too cold.

Regardless, Tiffanie waded right into that water, then transformed herself into what looked like a mermaid. The kind of mermaid *without* a little shell brassiere.

She started singing.

Larry clapped his wren wings over his ears and proclaimed her siren song was so absolutely wrong it hurt, but I thought her voice was the most beautiful I'd ever heard. Her voice, or the words, or her voice and the words and the melody together were soothing and enticing and full of the promise of something just beyond articulating but highly desirable. I don't know how else to describe it except it was like knowing there's a piece of your favorite kind of chocolate sitting on the kitchen counter, and you're trying to keep to a diet so you haven't eaten anything except the good-for-you stuff in two weeks, and you know you're supposed to be in the other room, working on your five-page homework assignment, due tomorrow, comparing *Silas Marner* and *The Waste Land*, and you haven't read either because one is so boring and the other totally incomprehensible, so you're trying to skim through the Cliff's Notes, which themselves are boring and incomprehensible, and trying to come up with something to bluff your way through another four and three-quarters pages now that you've written your name, homeroom number, and, "In this paper, I will compare the novel *Silas Marner* by George Eliot and the poem *The Waste Land* by T. S. Eliot," and the piece of chocolate is *calling* you—by name—saying, "Come and eat me before somebody else does"— that's what Tiffanie's song was like.

The song somehow made me feel…oh, I don't know…like a worthwhile person: brave and self-sufficient and naturally gracious—all the things I wanted to be and admired in others but had always suspected I could only pretend to be. The kind of person whose father would not ditch her and move to Hong Kong, no matter how he felt about her mother. All I needed to do was listen to that song, and I would be that complete person. . . .

I came to my senses when I fell.

My hands smacked into the hard-packed sand, and that was the first I was aware I'd stood up from our hiding place behind the dune and had begun walking toward the shore. What had happened was that Brave Heart had grabbed the cuff of my jeans in his teeth and set his woolly butt down in the sand to hold me there.

Larry was flapping his wings in Eleni's face, which didn't seem to be doing much good about getting her attention as *she* started walking, wearing a dazed but happy expression on her face.

So Larry bit her nose.

"Ow!" Eleni finally stopped walking and rubbed her nose.

"Stick your fingers in your ears," Larry said. "You silly human girls seem susceptible to even Tiffanie's pathetic faux-mermaid warbling."

Wow. If that was fake, what would the real thing feel like?

Fingers in ears, we watched.

Down on the beach, one of the elves had come to the entryway of the cave. I waited for the other elves to join him, but none did. So maybe Larry was right, and we humans are easier to fool.

We had accounted for that in our plan: If all the elves came out, Tiffanie would lead them away while the rest of us went into the cave and released Julian and the dragon. But Tiffanie had warned that probably wouldn't happen, that she could imitate a siren song, but that it wouldn't be as potent as the real thing.

She kept on singing, and the lone elf kept on listening. Then, slowly, Tiffanie started swimming, parallel to the shore but toward where the beach curved away, out of sight of the cave. She'd told us that a real mermaid would be able to make the elves walk out into the water until they drowned, though a real mermaid wouldn't as they're friendly with elves. In any case, Tiffanie's song wouldn't be that powerful: Any elves who followed it would come to their senses—if not at the feel of the cold sea, at least when they started choking on the water.

"Good," Eleni had said. "We don't need to be killing anyone."

I wasn't quite sure how I felt about the idea of drowning—or of not being able to drown—our enemies. Which was not how that good, perceptive, self-confident person I wanted to be would feel. I realized the person I wanted to be was Eleni.

Now, though it meant leaving our ears unplugged, she and I grabbed up a stone each and took off running. I was mentally singing Christmas carols—the songs whose lyrics came most readily to mind—to block out the siren song. Brave Heart and Larry came with us, but Eleni and I were the ones who were going to have to act. My chest and stomach and head hurt from anticipation. It was one thing to think it would be easier for us if this guy drowned, it was another to bash him over the head.

We came up the beach behind the elf, still held captive by Tiffanie's singing and totally oblivious to us. We knew that we were supposed to knock him out.

How hard is hard enough? I wondered.

In the movies, people are always bonking other people on the head. Sometimes, like in murder mysteries, what looks like a minor tap results in accidental death. Other times, like in horror films, you have to keep bashing away, and then the person still gets up and comes after you.

I waited for Eleni to strike him first.

But she was holding back, waiting for me.

I'd never hit anyone before—not intentionally, not stronger than an elbow in my friend Shelley's ribs once in a while to get her attention when she was being particularly obnoxious about something. I'd once accidentally hit Nancy Jean in the back of the head with a copy of Strunk and White's *Elements of Style* that I was trying to toss to Anna behind her in study hall, but it's a paperback, and even then it's only about a hundred pages. Nancy Jean carried on about needing a paramedic to check her out, but she gave herself away because she specified she needed a handsome, *young* paramedic.

In the water, Tiffanie was making come-on-

what's-the-delay? gestures at us with her hands because the elf was too far away for her to use her stop-
action spell. Luckily, he still didn't turn around to
see us.

I looked at the stone in my hand. I wanted to just
throw the thing at the guy, but I know what my aim
is like: If I let go of the stone, I would have been
more likely to hit Eleni than the elf.

I drew my arm back.

Out of my peripheral vision, I saw Eleni draw her
arm back, too.

I swung.

Eleni swung.

I missed entirely, somehow or other not being
close enough to him.

Eleni closed her eyes at the last second, and lost
track of where she was aiming. She gave his ear a
good, hard clip.

The elf staggered, but at the same time whirled
around. He went for his sword, which—we lucked
out—he didn't have with him, as he must have taken
it off to sit down for his meal.

But he did have a knife, which he now whipped
out, and—equally dangerous—I saw him open his
mouth to call out a warning to the others back at the
cave.

A bundle of snarling wool leaped past me and hit the elf in the chest, knocking him backward, flat on his back on the ground. Brave Heart stood on the elf's chest, looking much more menacing than a fuzzy ball of high-grade sweater should.

The elf had not only had the breath knocked out of him, he had dropped the knife, and Eleni dashed in to swoop it up from the ground, which I thought was incredibly brave of her.

"Twitch, and I'll slit your throat," she said, and he had no way of knowing what an empty threat that was.

I knelt on the ground on the other side of him, holding a big rock over his head as though seriously considering knocking his brains out, which I thought was incredibly brave of *me*. "Good Fluffy," I told Brave Heart. All the while what I wanted to do was shout out: *My grandma kicks butt!*

Tiffanie waded back to shore. Despite the fact that it was only us and an enemy elf present, she had made herself look like the gorgeous elf shepherdess again. Like the gorgeous *dry* elf shepherdess, though the perfectly arranged hair was obviously an illusion since *something* was dripping seawater onto me. Tiffanie held her hand up in traffic cop fashion, and the elf froze.

Larry took the opportunity to land on the guy's forehead, where he did a happy dance along the lines of a football player who's scored the winning touchdown, and taunted the elf, calling him, "Sissy girl."

"Get those vines," Tiffanie ordered us, and Eleni and I scrambled to get enough to tie him up with. "And seaweed for his mouth."

Yuck.

I could tell when she let go of the spell, for he struggled against his bindings, though we had him so tightly wrapped he obviously wasn't going anywhere. Larry finally flew off his face and onto Eleni's shoulder, and Fluffy the attack sheep finally uncurled his snarl and stepped off the elf's chest.

"Don't make me regret not killing you," Tiffanie told the elf, and that settled him a bit.

She gave a tired *huff* and I was reminded, yet again, that no matter what she looked like and no matter what her magic powers were, she was an old, wet, tired lady.

And we still had five more elves to get out of the way.

To say nothing of the dragon.

23

A Sheep in Wolf's Clothing

art two of our plan started with Tiffanie changing Brave Heart's appearance from Fluffy the sheep to the kind of wolf who would eat Little Red Riding Hood, her grandmother, *and* the woodcutter.

"Run fast," Tiffanie reminded him for about the fifth time, "because elves are legendary in their skill with the bow. But don't run *too* fast, because we don't want them giving up the chase and coming back here. Besides, I've got to be able to keep up, too, just in case you get in trouble."

Brave Heart, who seemed besotted with her, licked her hand, and Tiffanie crouched down to hug him.

Then she turned to me. *Obviously* to talk, not to hug. "Your turn," she said, but if that was supposed to give me enough time to brace myself, it only gave me enough time for my stomach to tighten. The spell crept over me, like a hundred cats giving me a tongue-bath.

I looked down at myself and saw that I'd turned as black as...well, as black as a shadow, which is what I was supposed to be. It was disconcerting because I was still three-dimensional, the spell being only a glamour, but Tiffanie assured me that in the cave, lit only by witchlight, I would melt into the... uhm, shadows.

Eleni hugged me. "Be careful," she whispered.

Since Larry was still perched on her shoulder, he overheard the concern in her voice, and he chimed in with advice of his own: "Don't do anything stupid." He seemed to decide that was too much to ask of me and added, "If you can help it."

Tiffanie, showing more warmth for me than usual, asked, "You still here?" and wiggled her fingers for me to go.

I crept across the sand dunes. Literally. That way, if any of the remaining elves happened to glance out of the cave—like, for example, to say, *Hey, I wonder whatever happened to old what's-his-name who left to follow the mermaid song?*—they wouldn't spot a big, standing-up-in-the-air, girl-shaped shadow striding toward them. If I was on the ground, we hoped they wouldn't notice me at all; and if they did see me, horizontal rather than vertical, the idea was that they would take my shape for the shadow of one of the scrubby beach bushes, which I was supposed to try to stay near—even though that just about doubled the time I was spending out in the open—or of one of the clouds scudding overhead.

Larry was my lookout. Still in the form of a wren, he flew nearby so that he could keep an eye on the cave entrance while I kept my head down and concentrated on crawling. If he spotted any of the elves, he was supposed to call out a warning, and I would stop moving and flatten myself into the sand.

I was grateful that, when they'd come up with this plan, Eleni had told Tiffanie about how I'd hurt my knee when I'd fallen off the curb in 1953. Tiffanie had done a spell—which felt sort of like rubbing a banana peel on my knee—and my knee had been healed. In about five seconds. With only the faintest scar. The sand was gritty enough on my skin. Even the thought of it grinding into an open wound hurt.

Larry chirped like a wren and I flattened.

Then I heard, close by, a long, loud wolf howl.

Even expecting it, I got goose bumps. Brave Heart made a much more convincing wolf than a sheep.

I finally raised my eyes and saw that Larry hadn't been warning that the elves were watching, but had been letting me know I had reached the side of the cliff wall whose front had the huge crack that formed the cave entrance. Basically, Larry had been saying good-bye. Thanks for the heart attack, Larry. And he'd flown back to tell the others I was in position. We'd already spotted a scrubby little tree coming out of the rock right by the opening and decided that would make a good hiding place. I stood bent at an angle in its shadow, pressing myself against the cliff wall, hoping no one would notice what a fat shadow that little tree cast.

Brave Heart howled again.

I couldn't help myself: I tipped my head slightly to see him sitting on the crest of the sand dune we'd hid behind earlier, his head thrown back, howling at the sun rather than at the moon. Very impressive.

I heard the elves falling all over themselves to get to the cave opening, to learn what was going on. It was a wide opening, with more than enough room for the three who clustered there. Berrech wasn't among them, nor did any of them look old enough to be Berrech's father, Vediss.

Come on, you slugs, I thought. *Investigate. Step away from the cave.*

From inside, someone—Vediss, I guessed, because I thought I'd recognize Berrech's voice—asked, incredulous, "A wolf? Here?"

Tiffanie had explained that dragons and wolves do not get along well enough to share territory, and that there shouldn't be wolves anywhere near Dragons' Cove. Apparently the elves knew this, too.

"Yeah," one of the others said. "Staggering about like it's sick."

That had been part of Brave Heart's instructions. Healthy wolves don't normally prey on humans or elves, but there was no telling what a diseased wolf might do.

One of the three elves went back into the cave and came back out with a bow and arrows; but, anticipating this, Brave Heart had slipped back below the crest of the dune. He howled again.

"It's gone," one of the three complained.

"Might come back," said the one with the bow. "Might sneak up on us unawares."

They had a minor discussion. Now I did hear Berrech, though from where I was hiding I couldn't see him. He asked about someone and was told he'd "gone off chasing a mermaid." This did not amuse

Berrech who, it sounded like, didn't approve of much, including mermaids.

"Frivolous nonsense," he muttered. Then he said, "All right," and named one of them, "you go and track that wolf."

We'd been hoping at least two would go, and fortunately one of the elves must have been getting the cave equivalent of cabin fever, for he pointed out that it's always wise for two to hunt together "in case of eventualities."

"All right, all right," Berrech grumbled, in bad humor. "Though that leaves few of us here—'in case of eventualities.'"

The voice that had to be Vediss's tried to calm him. "No one knows about this place," he soothed his son. "No one will be coming here. Come, let us finish."

The elf with the bow and the elf who wanted to accompany him took off across the dunes.

In theory, Larry should have been somewhere in the vicinity of the dune but watching the cave, to warn Brave Heart that the elves were on the move. Unfortunately, Larry was too small for me to see from this distance—even with my new, improved Kazaran Dahaani eyesight—so I could only hope he hadn't wandered off looking for spreenie amusements elsewhere.

I heard Brave Heart howl, and it sounded as though he'd taken off, so that was a good sign. If they got the chance, he and Tiffanie would get the two elves separated and lost.

The third elf lingered at the cave entrance until his companions disappeared over the sand dune, then turned back into the cave.

At the same moment, I slipped in around the edge of the entry so that, if anyone noticed, they would assume I was his shadow.

I was in the cave.

So far, so good.

Except...

Why is there always an *except*?

As I slid into the cave, keeping my back to the wall, I saw that Larry's descriptions had been mostly accurate. Glowing globes that looked like frozen snowballs were scattered liberally about the cave, and gave a good deal of light but also cast a lot of shadows: Think Christmas midnight Mass. The cave itself was about as big as a good-sized classroom, and I glimpsed, in the back, trying hard *not* to see it and let myself become overwhelmed, a large form that had to be the dragon, lying on the floor like someone's pet brontosaurus. It raised its head the instant I crossed the threshold. I told myself that was just coincidence.

I even glimpsed, near where the dragon's eyes were tracking me, the glint of bars—the cage Larry had said Julian was being kept in.

But I didn't bother looking any closer. *Larry, you blue fool,* I thought, for I saw Julian sitting at the table with an older elf who had to be Vediss. Vediss had what looked like a permanent scowl—an expression like his underwear was too loose while simultaneously his pants were too tight. Julian was cool and unperturbed, wearing a pair of familiar-looking shades.

And Vediss was telling him, "Good, good. You'll take those fools totally by surprise."

24

The Plan: Part II, Stage C...
or Was That Part III, Stage A?
Or...Never Mind

ou traitor, I thought. *We're risking our lives to rescue you from Vediss, and here you are working with him all along.*

But that didn't make any sense.

Vediss and Berrech wanted Julian out of the way of the kingship. If Julian didn't want to succeed his father, all he had to do was step aside for Berrech; he didn't need to plot with him. And where was Berrech, anyway? I'd heard his voice, but he wasn't here at the table with his father, nor at the other table where the last of his henchmen was sitting down to finish his meal.

The dragon got to its feet, rattling the short but

236

thick chains that looped from some massive bolts in the cave wall to the heavy collar tight around its neck, so that the creature had room to sit or stand but little other movement. It could definitely see me, I could tell, even though it pretended to be just stretching.

He tried to make wren fricassee out of me, I remembered Larry saying. Wren fricassee or human-girl-disguised-as-shadow fricassee: Gee, if I were a dragon, which would I prefer?

His fire breath can't reach this far, I told myself, *or he could have had elf fricassee.*

I heard Berrech's voice call to the dragon, "No trouble out of you, now."

Berrech's voice, coming from Julian's mouth.

The dragon yawned, then lay down again, capturing my attention, making me see him, and—beyond him—the cage Larry had described. The cage in which Julian was held prisoner. Though the dragon had seen me, Julian had not. He was leaning against the back set of bars, looking desolate, looking—truth be told—a bit sorry for himself.

The Julian at the table said, in Berrech's voice, "These things hurt my ears." He took the glasses off and didn't look anything like Julian anymore. How could I have been mistaken? Berrech was bigger than

Julian in every way—taller, wider, broader features—and his hair was darker and longer.

Vediss chose a small pair of pliers from among the tools on the table, and he made an adjustment to the frames. "Put them back on," he said. "You have to get used to leaving them on, even when you enter an ill-lit room. Even though they look as though they're made to block out light, you can wear them in the dark."

Berrech put the glasses back on, and his features once more resumed the shape of Julian's in Julian's human-boy mode.

I finally caught on. These glasses were not a replacement pair for the ones that had ended up on my front lawn, which had let the wearer see things as they actually were; but they were a whole new magic, where it was those on the other side of the lenses who were affected.

The dragon began licking its forelegs, cleaning itself or perhaps smoothing down its scales, like a cross between a house cat and an armored tank. It glanced up at me as though to say, *See, I'm domesticated. I'm friendly.*

And in truth it had already proven its friendliness by not drawing the elves' attention to me, by—in fact—drawing my attention to Julian.

Intelligent, I reminded myself. What had Tiffanie said? Able to plan. Able to hold grudges.

It didn't need me to explain that we'd rescue it if it helped us. It was volunteering.

I weighed the options of once again crawling on the floor versus remaining upright and hugging the irregular walls of the cave. The advantage of crawling was that it made me a smaller target; the advantage of being upright was that I could keep a better eye out for Vediss or Berrech glancing in my direction so I could freeze at a moment's notice. The other factor I had to throw into the equation was the question of how long I could move around the cave in either position before I knocked into something.

And thinking about time reminded me that I didn't have long before Eleni would get moving into her role in this plan—which was striking me as more and more lame by the minute. How many minutes had I dawdled in here already?

I opted for impersonating the shadow of the Hunchback of Notre Dame—standing, though crookedly, so that my shape merged as much as possible into the real shadows thrown by the crates and equipment and buckets of sand that Vediss had in here for his glassmaking experiments.

To anyone watching—which, hopefully, was just

the dragon—I would have looked like a spastic Quasimodo. Once I passed the tables where the elves sat, I kept glancing forward in the direction I was heading, to lessen the probability of tripping over something. Then I would quickly glance back to make sure Vediss and Berrech were still occupied, then twitch my head to the side to make sure the other elf wasn't looking, then forward again. Whiplash was a real possibility.

Still, my precautions were worthwhile, for I caught the moment when Berrech's head jerked up. Luckily, he was facing the entrance, so in the time it took for his head to swivel in my direction, I'd crouched and frozen.

Had I made a noise?

"What?" his father asked.

Berrech stood, and turned his eyes toward my end of the cave. But at least he didn't go for his sword. Nor come any closer. For the time being.

His father repeated, "What?"

"Don't know," Berrech said. "The lights flickered. Or at least one of them."

Now all three elves were looking in my basic direction. The henchman elf started toward me.

Stupid, stupid, I chided myself. I'd stepped between them and one of the globes of light as though I were as insubstantial as I was supposed to look.

The dragon flicked its tail, which it hadn't done before, aiming it so that it passed in front of one of the witchlights, and this time I noticed the slight flicker. The creature wore a smug expression as if trying to keep from grinning outright, like it was pleased that it had done something which had caused the elves to jump. Then, as though suddenly realizing that they were watching, it tucked its tail beneath itself. Speaking in a voice that somehow reminded me of lava bubbling out from a volcano (not, of course, that I've ever personally *heard* lava bubbling out from a volcano), the dragon suggested, "Perhaps one of you passed gas that caused a momentary dimming of the lights?"

Vediss wasn't the only one who could scowl like his shorts were caught somewhere they shouldn't be. Berrech said: "You may be about to outlive your usefulness, worm."

Worm? I thought. *Geez, he doesn't like anybody besides other elves—and he doesn't like half of them, either.*

"If you're going to kill me anyway," the dragon said, still slow and steady, like a geologic force, "then what will I lose by incinerating you now?" Suddenly, gracefully—despite all that mass and those short chains—it was on its feet, and it shot a blowtorchlike flame out of its mouth, between the advancing hench-elf and where Berrech and Vediss stood. On the table where the elves had been eating, what was left of their meal went up like flaming cherries jubilee.

The two thoughts that collided in my head were:

(1) Larry's pathetic little spreenie-trying-to-make-a-dragon-*whoosh* sounded just about nothing like the real thing; and

(2) Very precise aim!

The hench-elf put his little elf butt into reverse. A moment later he went and fetched a pail of sand that he threw onto the table to smother the flames before the table as well as the food started burning, but we all knew that hadn't been the first thought to cross his mind.

Vediss was trying to make peace. "Now, now, dragon. No reason to talk like that. Of course we aren't planning to kill you. I gave my word we would let you go when we finished, and we will. My son was only speaking in hasty irritation. Bear in mind that the situation is as it ever was since I captured you: If you kill us, with no one knowing you're here, you'll have starved to death by the time the other dragons find you next laying season. Starving is such a long death."

No wonder the poor creature was willing to work for them, on the off chance that they might let it live.

The dragon whipped its tail around itself and once more settled down with its chin on its paws. Waiting. We could all tell it was waiting.

Me, too: I waited for the elves to settle down, to stop stealing glances in the dragon's direction and, therefore, in mine.

My knees were beginning to stiffen. If I didn't move soon, my legs were apt to fall asleep and be unsteady. I eased myself up the wall, bending to follow the contours eroded eons ago by the sea when the tides had come in higher up the shore.

From outside the cave came a bloodcurdling scream.

I gasped, remembering—even as I did—that it was part of the plan.

Fortunately, everyone else gasped at the same time—minus the imperturbable dragon, of course—so no one noticed me.

"Wolf!" Though she was outside, Eleni's voice reverberated in the cave. "Wolf! Wolf! Somebody please help me!" This was followed by a scream so frightened and tormented it sounded as though she was even now having major body parts torn off.

Too late.

Or too early.

Depending on if you meant me or Eleni. I was supposed to have talked to the dragon and/or Julian by now. I was supposed to have found a key to unlock the iron collar and/or the cage. I was supposed to use this distraction to quickly unlock *something or other.*

Vediss, Berrech, and the remaining elf scrambled for their weapons.

The dragon, in a whisper so intense it smoked, hissed at me, "The shelf."

Shelf?

It nodded its massive head at a piece of board, on the far side of the cave from me, balanced on two crates.

Keys. A ring with two keys.

There was no time for skulking about. The elves were as distracted as the plan called for them to be. I dashed across the open floor to the shelf and snatched up the ring.

But old habits die hard.

I glanced back to make sure nobody was watching. The hench-elf and Vediss were not in sight, presumably having already made it outside to investigate what was making Eleni continue to scream. Berrech had his back to me and was just about to step through the cave entryway when Larry swooped in.

NOW YOU SEE IT . . .

Larry didn't see Berrech.

Or, rather, Larry didn't see Berrech as Berrech—since he was still wearing those form-confusing glasses. He appeared, to anyone who didn't know better, to be Julian.

In the chaos of someone being attacked, Berrech probably wouldn't have noticed a little wren.

Except that the wren hovered, very unwrenlike, in his face and spoke.

With all of Eleni's screaming, I couldn't hear what Larry said, but it must have been something like: *Julian, we're here to rescue you.*

Berrech skidded to a stop. Gaped at the wren. Then swiveled around to check out Julian, who had gotten to his feet at the sound of all that disturbance and was standing clutching the bars of the cave, watching him.

The next place Berrech's gaze landed was on me.

25

Einstein's Theory of Relativity Didn't Include *Bad* Relatives

My brain seemed to be working at something like the speed of light, but my motor control didn't seem to be working at all.

Berrech pulled out a knife and flung it at me. It was heading straight for my face with me knowing there was no way I could drop to the ground in time to avoid it.

Which is no reason for you to stand there like a bulls-eye waiting for it, I told myself.

But as the knife sped toward me, I couldn't even close my eyes.

Which was okay, because then I would have

missed the moment when the dragon incinerated it midair.

The dragon must have been able to sniff out my real species; either that or something about my shadow shape labeled me as human, not elf or any of the other choices possible in this world. In any case, in the moment it took Berrech to realize his weapon had not killed me but was settling to the ground in a fine ash, the dragon called to me, "Human girl, will you be more or less inclined to unlock these chains if I cremate that elf?"

"No!" Julian cried. "Don't!" Then squinting in my direction he guessed, "Wendy?" and explained, "He's my kinsman."

The dragon wasn't interested in Julian's opinion and was watching me. From my position on the floor, where I'd finally dropped to make myself a smaller target, I figured, *C'mon, Julian, he's your cousin, but besides using me for target practice, he's been threatening to cut you into pieces.* All in all, the kind of guy who gives relatives a bad name.

Larry, seeing what looked like two Julians—one of whom was flinging sharp, pointed objects at me—picked up on the fact that something was wrong. Larry did what Larry did best: He shot out of that cave faster than a carnival's human cannonball.

Berrech was striding across the cave to come get me, but—much as I *didn't* want him to get me—I couldn't bring myself to tell the dragon, *Yeah, all right, barbecue him.*

"Try not to," I told the dragon.

The dragon, looking deeply disappointed in my decision, blasted flame not at Berrech, but at the worktable which stood between him and us.

Berrech took a hasty step back. Actually, many hasty steps back, until one more step would have taken him out of the cave altogether. "Father!" he yelled. "Merrindin! It's a trick! Get back in here!"

I popped up just long enough to grab the keys off the shelf suspended between the two crates. In the interest of time, since the flames that were keeping Berrech at bay were already subsiding, I called, "Julian, catch!" and flung the keys with such precision he would have needed an arm about six feet long to catch them.

The dragon, never taking its gaze off Berrech, said in its deep, grumbly voice, "Remember this," and swung its tail across the floor, sweeping the keys to within Julian's reach.

Julian got the cage door open just as the two other elves—Berrech's father, Vediss, and the elf whose name, apparently, was Merrindin—came back into the cave. Merrindin dragged Eleni with him, forcing her ahead of him as a shield, the blade of his knife under her chin.

Oh no, I thought. *Oh no, oh no, oh no.* And that was without even making it as far as thinking that if she died, I would cease to exist.

"Drop the keys," Berrech ordered Julian, "or the girl's death is on your hands."

Eleni still wore Tiffanie's elf shepherdess glamour, and obviously nobody knew who she was, but it had to be pretty clear to everyone that the pretty elf shepherdess and the shadow were working together to rescue Julian. I saw her eyes scan the room. Saw the hopelessness in her expression when she found me in plain sight and realized I would not be jumping out of any corners to be of help.

Eleni pointed out what I was too afraid to admit to myself: "He'll kill me in any case."

"No," Vediss said, and I took it as a bad sign that it was Vediss, and not Berrech, who offered that assurance.

The dragon apparently decided I had no more to offer at this point and shifted its attention to Julian. "Unchain me and I can make them pay for her death and get you out of here before the others return." When Julian didn't respond, the dragon said, "We can bring the human girl disguised as a shadow, too"—then, hedging its bets, added, "if you want."

"No," Julian said, soft as a sigh.

But before I could think, *It's been fun knowing you, too,* he said to the elves, "Let the girls go, and I'll surrender without a fight," and I realized he was refusing the dragon's offer in its entirety.

"You'll surrender in any case," Berrech said.

Julian had to know that Eleni and I were less than useless to Berrech and that we were already as good as dead, and that he probably was, too, and that his best chance was the dragon. But he let the keys drop to the floor.

Now it was the dragon's turn to sigh, a smoky, bubbling-lava sound.

I could knock over one of these crates of sand, I thought, *and have the dragon ignite it, sending molten glass oozing across the floor. . . .*

On the other hand, *oozing* is not a real dynamic split-second-timing, escape-type word. And oozing where? Toward Eleni?

Then, apparently, the dragon decided:

(a) There was no reason it should be bound by elven scruples; or

(b) It had nothing to lose; or maybe

(c) Both.

It opened its jaws wide and directed a blast of furnace flames at the elves.

"No!" I screamed, for one of those elves still held my grandmother.

Even if the dragon would have heeded me—and there was no reason why it should—my voice was lost in the sound of the rush of fire.

It wasn't my love for my grandmother or second thoughts by the dragon that spared her—it was a matter of the mathematics of force, velocity, and distance: The elves were beyond the dragon's range. Just barely.

Of course, they didn't immediately know that.

Startled, they flinched. They recoiled.

They stopped paying close attention to Eleni.

Eleni jabbed her elbow into Merrindin's side and at the same time twisted away from the knife he'd let dip away from her throat. He staggered, off balance, and she got her leg behind his and swept it out from under him so that he fell, flat on his back, pulling her down, with her landing on top of him, the knife clattering harmlessly to the floor.

Berrech and Vediss were so busy dodging the flames that hadn't reached them, they didn't notice what had happened until Eleni was scrambling to her feet, supporting her weight with her hand shoved deep into Merrindin's stomach. Fortunately, he was too dazed from cracking his head on the ground to put up a fight.

"Can't catch me!" Eleni taunted, just to make sure they were aware of her escaping, then she dashed out of the cave to draw them—I knew her well enough to guess her reasoning—away from me.

"Stop her!" Berrech ordered—maybe Merrindin or maybe his father. But since Merrindin wasn't moving, just rolling around a bit moaning, it was Vediss who took off after her.

Julian, meanwhile, had covered the distance from the back of the cave to the cave entrance in what had to be a world record, and launched himself onto Berrech, even as Berrech picked up Merrindin's fallen knife.

Scooping the keys off the floor, I told the dragon, "*You* remember *this.*"

And all the while I was thinking *I'm standing next to a dragon. I'm letting a dragon loose.* I wondered if it would feel indebted to us and stick around to help more, or if it would figure it had already helped enough and just light out of there, or if it would be ticked off at all the inept dithering that had gone on and take out its frustrations on all of us.

I got the collar loose, and the dragon surged forward.

Julian rolled out of the way—hard to tell if he saw or heard the dragon coming, or if that was just a natural move in his struggle with the knife-wielding Berrech. Whichever, it left a momentary opening for the dragon, who seized hold of Berrech, its huge claw covering his entire back, its talons spread from the elf's shoulders to his waist but not—at least for the moment—puncturing him. The dragon shook Berrech with obvious glee, sending the glasses flying.

Berrech—once again looking like himself— screamed, but I figured that had to be in terror, not pain, for the dragon obviously could have squeezed the life out of him in a heartbeat.

We all came stumbling out of the cave: the dragon holding on to Berrech, with Julian and I directly behind, tripping over Merrindin, who—despite the knock on the head—retained enough sense to know when it was time to just stay put. That time was when the dragon leaned its face close and hissed in a whisper of volcanic steam, "Don't even think about standing up."

On the beach outside, we saw that Vediss had caught up to Eleni but was having trouble holding on to her. Part of the problem was that she was flailing and kicking. But another distraction Vediss faced was that there was a brave little wren who—woodpecker-like—kept attacking the back of his head.

Just then Brave Heart the wolf came tearing over the crest of one of the sand dunes. Fur bristling, fangs gleaming, he obviously was intent on hurling himself at Vediss.

The dragon beat him to it, and grabbed Vediss in a similar hold to the one he had on Berrech.

Brave Heart spun around, sending sand flying, but he didn't have to go back for Tiffanie: She was just straggling into view. She slowed down when she saw everything was under control—more or less—and the measure of her exhaustion was that she let all our glamours fall away—including her own, so that she was back to looking like a hundred-year-old witch who had just spent the last fifteen minutes running up and down the hilly beach.

Over the dunes, the two elves who had been hunting Brave Heart came into sight. They took one look at us—or rather, they took one look at the dragon, and tore back over those dunes even faster than they had come.

Julian had his left hand tight on his right forearm, and the stupid thought crossed my mind that he was taking his pulse, which I thought was pretty superfluous, but then I saw the blood running down his arm and I realized maybe he hadn't been winning that scuffle with Berrech over the knife.

I still had Eleni's handkerchief, which she had given me for my knee, and I took it out of my pocket. "Very unsanitary, I know," I pointed out to him, as it had my blood on it, but I figured a risk of germs was better than his bleeding to death in front of me.

"Thank you," he said, still breathing hard as I tightened the makeshift bandage around his arm.

I hadn't realized until then that I apparently have a weakness for sweaty, bleeding elves who have just recently saved me from never being born.

Sweaty, bleeding *gracious* elves, I realized as soon as Tiffanie finally reached us.

She put her hand on his arm, and the flow of blood, which my pathetic attempt at helping had only slowed down, now stopped. Beneath the bandage, his wound had no doubt disappeared as entirely as the one on my knee that Tiffanie had healed. Much more useful than my silly already-used handkerchief.

Julian pulled her in closer to him and rested his chin on her head while she burrowed her face into his chest. "The spreenie said you were in trouble," she managed to gasp between gulps for air.

"The spreenie," corrected the spreenie-in-question, "said *Eleni* was in trouble."

I felt bad that I'd assumed the worst of Larry—that he had abandoned us, when in reality he'd gone to fetch help—but I didn't feel bad enough to apologize.

Larry fluttered his little blue eyelashes at my grandmother, and she took a second to say, "Thank you, Larry," on her way to come give me a hug.

I found myself clinging to her. "I thought...," I started.

"I know," she murmured. "But we're all fine."

With my eyes closed and my face buried in her hair, her voice was the same as it had always been, the comforting and gentle tone my grandmother used when I'd fallen off my tricycle, or when I was upset with my mother, or when Gia had had some success that made me feel insignificant.

Another voice, one like the shifting of tectonic plates, grumbled and grated, "If I may intrude..."

The dragon was still holding on to Vediss and Berrech.

I glanced at Julian and saw the easy, familiar way he and Tiffanie stood side by side with their arms around each other, despite the fact that he was looking his most attractive and she was sporting her

Wicked Witch of the West look. Just when I'd found myself getting interested. It served me right. Those troublesome assumptions about the way people look. It explained, if I had stopped to think about it, her frantic single-mindedness to rescue him. And if she loved him that much, that had to count for a lot and of course would be more meaningful than a few warts and wrinkles.

The dragon said to me, "I am indebted to you." It may have been holding Julian's uncle and cousin, but it was waiting for me. I'd been the one to actually undo those locks. In its mind, that made me the only significant one there. "I realize these are somehow related to your friend and that you are hesitant to see their blood shed, but they have held me prisoner for many weeks now."

Either the direction this was heading made Berrech and Vediss nervous, or the dragon in its agitation tightened its grip a bit, for they began to squirm, though it was obvious they were going nowhere.

"I could," the dragon offered, having to raise its voice to be heard over their pleas, "take them away so you wouldn't actually have to watch..."

"No," Julian said. "Please spare them." That plea seemed directed at both of us.

Now there was a wild thought: me and a dragon comprising an "us."

To Berrech and Vediss, Julian said, "I am tempted." That admission seemed to uncover the feelings he must have buried during his capture and kept under control until now. He spat out the words, "I am *so* tempted."

Sounding worried, Tiffanie started, "But you—"

Julian spoke over her. "But I cannot begin my public career with the death of my kinsmen." He stood there looking so furious I wondered if he was hoping one of us would find a flaw in his reasoning and point out how he *could* let the dragon eat them. But then he took a steadying breath and spoke to the dragon. "I realize you have suffered at their hands, that you have been held against your wishes and been in fear for your life."

We could all tell by the grumbling going on in the dragon's chest and throat that this was going nowhere toward making it feel inclined toward leniency. "Yes...?" the dragon prompted, a bit of steam escaping its jaws.

Julian hesitated.

I could see Tiffanie's gnarled fingers dig into his arm, but she didn't say anything.

Finally Julian said, "But in the end, they did not

harm you. I will bring this up before the High Council, and they will not take any of this lightly. These two, as the leaders, will be imprisoned, and to an elf that is great punishment."

The captive elves nodded vigorously, obviously much favoring elf justice over dragon justice.

The dragon's internal grumbling continued, and it narrowed its eyes at Julian.

Eleni, holding my hand, gripped it tighter.

Brave Heart barked. And barked and barked.

Tiffanie listened. And after a while, she smiled. "You are truly wise," she told the dog. For the rest of us, she interpreted. "Brave Heart points out that at his home there is a saying: 'Who is the pet, and who is the master, and who has trained whom?'"

Larry, once again sitting on Eleni's shoulder, clapped his little blue hands over his chest and declared, "Oooo, that's deep," which was kind of along the lines of what I'd been thinking—which was, *Huh?*—but at least I'd had the sense not to say it.

"Quiet, spreenie," Tiffanie ordered. To the dragon she said, "These elves must have provided you with food in the time while they held you prisoner."

The elves interrupted to remind the dragon of all their efforts on behalf of its comfort.

Tiffanie talked over them: "And, as a logical consequence of feeding generally comes…"

"Never these two in particular," the dragon said. "But they assigned their underlings…" The dragon caught on, as I did. The cave was not *that* big, and if the elves were to share it with a dragon that couldn't go out, someone must have done a fair amount of shoveling. And of course Berrech and Vediss would consider themselves above such a task.

There was a noise which I thought was the beginnings of an earthquake, but it was the dragon laughing. "The Dragon Warrens could use a certain amount of cleaning," it said. "After all these generations. It might take five or six or seven years. But I could return them to you when they have finished." It asked me, "Does this meet with your approval?"

I checked by glancing at Julian, who was watching Tiffanie. She nodded, then he did, so I did, too.

Berrech and his father did their best to look grateful, though they may well have been having second thoughts.

"Thank you," I said. And because the formal language Julian and the dragon had been using had me kind of caught up in it, I found myself saying, "I may have saved your life, but you also saved mine, and that of my…kinswoman, Eleni. Our lives are now twined together, and I will remember—I will ever remember—your kindness."

That, I told myself even as the words left my mouth, *was not well thought out.* I had just, basically, told a dragon to feel free to give me a call.

The dragon looked startled, but didn't laugh at me. It bowed its head in what appeared to be all earnestness.

I bowed back.

And in that instant while I wasn't looking, it took to the air, carrying the two elves with it.

26

Letting Go

As soon as the dragon was gone, Merrindin got to his feet and broke for the dunes.

"Never mind," Tiffanie told Brave Heart, who had made to lunge in that direction. "We know who he is, as well as the other two."

"Three," Eleni corrected, remembering the mermaid-chasing one we'd left tied up with vines and seaweed.

"Three," Tiffanie said. "They'll all be spending a good long time in public service for what they've done. Dragons aren't the only creatures who need cleaning up after."

So that, all of a sudden, was the end of that.

In the chaos of trying to come up with plans

without knowing exactly what was going on; of facing dangers involving all sorts of potential for catastrophe, including but not limited to imminent death; of getting to meet my grandmother as a teenager, then growing to enjoy her company as a brave and funny and fiercely loyal friend rather than as an elderly relative, I had . . . not exactly *forgotten,* but . . . *put aside* the thought of what awaited me back home.

Back at the *nursing* home.

Now that knowledge simultaneously filled me and left me empty.

Such nuances of emotional devastation were beyond Tiffanie. "These two will never be able to find their way back without help," she told Julian as though Eleni and I were not people with ears—and feelings—but two fruit baskets that needed to be sorted out and delivered. "I'll take *her*"—she indicated Eleni—"because that will give me the chance to talk to Brave Heart's humans to see if I can buy him from them." For those of us not fluent in Dog, she explained that even while she and Brave Heart were running up and down the dunes confusing the elves, they had discussed this and that Brave Heart:

(1) absolutely wanted to go with her; and

(2) was under the impression his owners would be happy to sell him, since he had

grown considerably bigger than the pet-store owner had led them to believe; and

(3) offered that, should they need extra convincing, he could always start chewing slippers and peeing on the rug.

Brave Heart barked so enthusiastically that we all became, suddenly, fluent in Dog.

"I'll go with you," Larry announced. He pointed at the three of them in turn—Eleni, Brave Heart, and Tiffanie—naming them: "Beauty and the Beast and the Beast."

"Who invited you?" Tiffanie snarled at him. To me, she said, "See you back in Mrs. Robellard's class." Then—being the sentimental person she is—added, "Tell anyone about any of this, and I'll turn you into a toad."

"Okay," I said. Eleni was looking as panicked as I felt about how quickly things were suddenly moving. I asked, "Why are we saying good-bye now when we have that long walk back through the forest to get to the gate?"

Tiffanie sighed, but Julian patiently explained, "There's another gate just over that rise. Normally the gates aren't built so close together, but once the dragons took over Dragons' Cove, this one became pretty much unusable, at least during fledgling season. But there's no reason we can't use it now."

So. We were out of time.

"Good-bye," I said to Tiffanie, because that was just for now, and—besides—she hated me, and I was afraid of her.

She gave a halfhearted wave, but mostly she was occupied with finding just the right glamour for herself, trying out different 1950s looks—all of them, of course, gorgeous.

Next came Brave Heart, because I'd known him the least amount of time. It should have been easier than it was. I knelt in the sand to give him a hug. "Good-bye, Brave Heart," I told him. "You *are* very well named."

He wasn't the kind of dog to hold a grudge. He gave me a slobbery dog kiss on the cheek.

Larry was noisily and wetly licking his lips all over and puckering up, but I figured a dog kiss was about as far as I was willing to go.

"One question, you little blue aberration," I said. "How did you happen to choose me?"

"Choose you?" Larry repeated, obviously reluctant to admit my train of thought had left the station without him.

"For the glasses." He was still pondering this, so I

spelled it out for him: "How did you come to choose me to give the glasses to after you stole them from Vediss? How did you know I would eventually help you, and therefore Julian?"

"Oh," Larry said. He shrugged his little iridescent wings and admitted, "I didn't. I just grabbed them then flung them through the nearest gate. I had no idea where they landed."

So much for being the ordained one. The Chosen One. She of Whom the Prophecies Speake.

"Good-bye, Larry," I said. "I'll think of you every time I lose a sock in the laundry."

"So long, kid," he told me. As he was suddenly talking out of the side of his mouth, I suspected he was doing an impersonation of somebody-or-other; I just didn't know who. He said: "Just remember this: We'll always have Paris." He blew a percussive kiss at me.

I didn't like the way he made it sound as though we'd shared some kind of special moments and worried what the others would think. But then I remembered they all knew Larry.

Eleni shooed him off her shoulder so the two of us could talk without him. "Take care, Jeannette," she told me, brushing my hair off my forehead, just the way she used to when I was a toddler.

"You, too." For the first time in hours I remembered that Jeannette is my mother's name. That there would come a time when my grandmother could not tell me and my mother apart. That there would come another time when she didn't know either one of us. There was so much to say, and I couldn't think how to say any of it. I blurted out, "You were so brave." Because that, of all qualities, is the hardest to fake.

She gave a dismissive snort. "You, too."

"No." I shook my head for emphasis. *Me?* Maybe to someone outside I might have looked like I did one or two gutsy things, but it wasn't because I was brave, it was because I was backed into a situation and wasn't smart enough to think of anything that could be done differently.

Eleni took hold of my chin and she forced me to look directly into her eyes, though I was trying to avoid this, because my eyes were suddenly wet. She said, "You fight the things you can fight. The rest you have to let go. That's all anyone can do."

She thought there was something *I* was afraid of, something *I* couldn't face.

"You, too," I insisted to her. What could I say: *Especially fifty years from now when you're fading away. Fight the Alzheimer's.* And how, exactly, could she do that?

She took my weeping the wrong way. She guessed: "We'll never meet again, will we?"

"Yes," I assured her wholeheartedly. "You'll see a lot of me. You will."

And that helped her.

But I knew *I* would never see *her* again, not in any way that counted.

She nodded at me, believing my true-but-only-as-far-as-it-went statement.

I nodded, too, then hugged her, and then let her go. Because there was nothing else I could do.

JULIAN CAME with me, returning me to the Westfall gardens a moment after I'd first passed through the gate. As soon as we were back, Tiffanie's spell that caused him to look human on Earth kicked in again; but now I knew how to look beyond that.

"Is she the one you visit here?" he asked. "Eleni?"

I nodded, mumbling, "She's my grandmother." My eyes were leaking again, and I expected him to have no patience with that, big warrior elf that he was, but he put his arm around my shoulders to steady me. It had the opposite effect.

He said, "There's so much of her in you. Not just the way you look, but your spirit, your honesty, your strength. It must be difficult for you, having her in this place."

Well, that killed any chance of my being able to stop crying anytime soon. Even if he was all wrong about me.

"She wouldn't give up on you," I told him, "but she's given up on herself."

Of course there was no way for him to know what, exactly, was going on—why Nana was in the nursing home. For all he knew, her body could be failing. A failing body was something I could understand.

He asked, "What do you mean?"

"How can you forget things that are really important to you?" I demanded. "I mean, I understand Alzheimer's makes it so you can't remember streets and you get lost, and you forget where you've put things, and you don't know what day it is. But how can someone forget her family? It's not like forgetting to bring home a book you need for a homework assignment, or like messing up the words to a poem you're supposed to have memorized. How can you forget love?" Before I knew what I was about to say, I blurted out: "It's just like a father deciding his life is more convenient without you."

"Oh, Wendy," Julian murmured, letting me hide my face in his chest. Though back on the beach in Kazaran Dahaani, he hadn't been standing close enough to hear when Eleni and I had been saying good-bye, his advice was close to hers: "Some things can't be fought."

"If this is your idea of comforting me, you're doing a stinky job." I pushed away from him and rubbed at my eyes, hating that I was making a fool of myself in front of him.

"She hasn't chosen this," Julian said. "Sometimes bravery and strength and goodness just aren't enough."

It wasn't like I was greedy. It wasn't like I expected she should live *forever*.

"And I don't know about your father, but I suspect that if he's chosen a life without you, it was not an easy choice; and it was probably not a choice *against* you, but *for* something else."

Sometimes, I reminded myself, you just have to let go.

I rubbed the tears away. I would do the right thing, I decided: I would forgive my father for choosing another woman over my mother and me; I would forgive my mother for choosing another man after my father and in addition to me; I would forgive my grandmother for leaving me; and I would forgive myself for not being the person I wanted to be, though I would try harder to *be* that person.

"Don't you ever get tired of being right all the time?" I muttered at him.

Then I blinked, surprised. "I can see."

He raised his eyebrows at me.

"No prescription glasses, no magical glasses: I shouldn't be able to see you, even this close up." I looked beyond him, and the trees were in focus, and the nursing home's back porch, and the nurse's aide who was standing there still glowering at us for running through here—thirty seconds ago, her time.

Julian said, "My mother must have done a healing spell on your vision."

"Your mother?" I demanded, that thought temporarily shoving aside the wonder that I had been wrong yet again, that Tiffanie had done something nice for me. "Tiffanie's your *mother?*"

Wearing a mild but inscrutable expression, Julian said, "Yes."

"But you're an elf."

"Half elf. That's one of the reasons Berrech is so offended at the thought of my succeeding my father." Now he was definitely holding back a grin. "Why? What did you think?"

"Never mind. Would she—could she help my grandmother?"

That wiped the grin off his face. "Oh, Wendy." I guessed his answer even before he said it: "Some things are too lost for even magic to bring back."

There was no use being angry at him. Or at life.

I flung my hair over my shoulder and strode up the path toward the back entrance.

"May I come with you?" he called.

I had assumed he would, but was even more pleased that he asked. I waved for him to catch up.

As we passed the nurse's aide, she reminded us in an aggrieved tone reminiscent of the dragon's grumbling, "No running."

We did our best to look penitent, at least until we got onto the elevator. Julian asked, "So Gia is your...?"

"Wicked stepsister," I supplied.

"Wicked?"

I shrugged and admitted, "Actually, she's okay, I guess. She's the daughter of my mother's current husband, Bill. He's not really half bad, either—never abandoned me in the woods or asked for my heart in a box or anything."

"Current," Julian repeated like he was having trouble keeping up with human thinking, though he'd had almost an entire school year of it, so maybe it was just me. "How many husbands has your mother had?"

"Just the two, my dad and Bill."

"Uh-huh."

"Surely that's not implied criticism I'm hearing in your tone," I said.

"Surely not," Julian agreed.

As long as I was going around forgiving people, I could certainly spare some forgiveness for Bill for not being Dad.

Julian and I walked into my grandmother's room together.

"Hello, Miss Lysiak," I said to her roommate, who fluttered a hand at us.

Gia was still sitting on the bed, the open photo album spread across her lap. "Hi, Julian," she said. "Hey, Wendy. Feeling better?"

Better? It took me a moment to remember how claustrophobic I'd been feeling—minutes ago, as far as Gia was concerned. How I had fled the room. I didn't know how I felt about her ability to read me like that, but I nodded to acknowledge her concern. "Better," I mumbled. "Thanks."

Better about some things, worse about others. I'd never thought of my grandmother as someone my age. Now it was even harder to lose her.

Gia closed the album, just as I saw she was still on the same page as when I'd left. I glimpsed the photo Eleni's friend Betsy had snapped on the street corner, Eleni wearing her blue and white gauzy dress, looking young, and fearless, and full of life. Gia stood and went to put the album away, to make room for all of us.

Finally, finally, I looked at my grandmother. She seemed intent on a piece of air about a foot and a half from her face.

Julian crouched down in front of her, took her hand, whispered the elven greeting, "Well met, Eleni," and kissed her fingertips.

No reaction at all.

I hesitated, patting her shoulder awkwardly. I forced myself to sit down next to her, to put away the anger I had not realized I'd been feeling, anger that she was leaving me, anger that she wasn't fighting to stay—even though I knew she *couldn't*. I buried my face into the crook of her neck and said what I hadn't said in years, since I'd been a little kid: "I love you, Nana."

Still no reaction.

For about five seconds.

Maybe it was the presence of Julian, whom she had not seen in half a century, maybe it was his calling her by her long-ago name, maybe it was my tears. Maybe, even, Tiffanie had tried and this was the best she could accomplish.

Nana sat just a little bit straighter; that was what attracted my attention. Then there was a flicker—a ghost—of a smile. She whispered, "Jeannette."

Then she disappeared back to wherever it was she kept her thoughts.

Gia had come back from the desk just in time to hear. "Jeannette is our mother's name," she explained to Julian. "Sometimes Nana gets confused."

Sometimes, I thought.

But not necessarily always.

EPILOGUE

OKAY. WELL, so I guess how seriously you're taken might have more to do with your attitude than with your name.

But I still wish I had a sexy name.

Vivian Vande Velde, like Wendy, has been traumatized with pairs of unfashionable glasses since the tender age of two. Despite her parents' assurances that she was "cute" in her glasses, twenty-twenty hindsight (and photographic evidence) suggest to her that their

judgment may have been clouded by the oldest corrective lens there is: love.

PAT BRUCATO

She spent her first paycheck on contact lenses.

Vivian Vande Velde is also the author of *Heir Apparent* (winner of the Anne Spencer Lindbergh Prize for Best Children's Fantasy Novel), *Never Trust a Dead Man* (winner of the Mystery Writers of America's Edgar Allan Poe Award for Best Young Adult Mystery), as well as *Wizard at Work, Smart Dog,* and many others. *Now You See It . . .* is her twenty-fourth book. It is the only one of her books in which the main character wears glasses.

This is no accident.